Ian shouldn't be thinking about bedding his client's daughter...

But Marie was so much more than that. She was 100-percent woman. A woman he'd already seduced. A woman he wanted to seduce again...

Without realizing it, Ian had backed Marie up until her bottom leaned against his glass desk. She held on to the blunted edge tightly with both hands and her small breasts moved with her sudden shortness of breath.

Ian realized he was having a little problem finding air himself. He eyed Marie's mouth, but he didn't kiss her. Instead he skimmed his hand down over her slender hip, lingering on the tender skin of her bare thigh, then slowly inched the material of her skirt up until her panties were revealed.

Oh, there was no thong for Marie Bertelli. Instead her underwear was cotton and white and sexier than any scrap of silk and lace known to man. It clung to her womanhood like only cotton could. And made his mouth water with the urge to lower himself to his knees and press his lips against the swollen flesh just underneath.

And one look in her eyes told him she wanted it just as much as he did....

Blaze™

Dear Reader,

We wholeheartedly believe that everyone has a bit of rebel in them. You know, that tiny voice that tells you to go ahead and eat that ice cream? Buy that piece of naughty lingerie? Makes you lust after a man you shouldn't have? Well, that's exactly what happens to our heroine Marie when she stumbles across fellow attorney Ian Kilborn, the last man on earth she should be tempting.

In *Going Too Far*, good-girl-to-the-bone Marie Bertelli wants a man to see her for who she truly is. It's not enough that her friends have found sizzling soul mates or that her family chases off her dates, she's delivered the ultimate professional blow when her father runs into a legal problem and hires Ian, Marie's first lover, rather than coming to her. So Marie sets out to prove she's the better person for the job. Only, once she crosses paths with Ian, she doesn't just want to read his legal briefs, she wants to get into them....

We hope you enjoy the last installment in our LEGAL BRIEFS miniseries. We'd love to hear what you think. Write to us at P.O. Box 12271, Toledo, OH 43613, or visit us online at www.toricarrington.com.

Here's wishing you happy—and hot—reading!

Lori & Tony Karayianni
aka Tori Carrington

Books by Tori Carrington

GOING TOO FAR

Tori Carrington

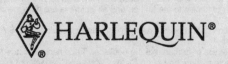

TORONTO • NEW YORK • LONDON
AMSTERDAM • PARIS • SYDNEY • HAMBURG
STOCKHOLM • ATHENS • TOKYO • MILAN • MADRID
PRAGUE • WARSAW • BUDAPEST • AUCKLAND

For our Greek brothers and sisters Katina and Georgos,
Andreas and Lambrini, Victoria and Alfon,
Theonesis and Dina, and Thotheres and Georgia,
whose enduring love proves that *happily ever after* aren't
merely words on a page. You inspire us.
Happy Valentine's Day!

ISBN 0-373-79077-5

GOING TOO FAR

Copyright © 2003 by Lori and Tony Karayianni.

All rights reserved. Except for use in any review, the reproduction or
utilization of this work in whole or in part in any form by any electronic,
mechanical or other means, now known or hereafter invented, including
xerography, photocopying and recording, or in any information storage
or retrieval system, is forbidden without the written permission of the
publisher, Harlequin Enterprises Limited, 225 Duncan Mill Road,
Don Mills, Ontario, Canada M3B 3K9.

All characters in this book have no existence outside the imagination of
the author and have no relation whatsoever to anyone bearing the same
name or names. They are not even distantly inspired by any individual
known or unknown to the author, and all incidents are pure invention.

This edition published by arrangement with Harlequin Books S.A.

® and TM are trademarks of the publisher. Trademarks indicated with
® are registered in the United States Patent and Trademark Office, the
Canadian Trade Marks Office and in other countries.

Visit us at www.eHarlequin.com

Printed in U.S.A.

1

MONDAYS HAD A WAY OF challenging even Marie Bertelli's good-girl tendencies. The weekend always seemed to go by too quickly. All too often the first day of the workweek seemed more like an ugly three-eyed monster to conquer rather than a fresh start to finish what she hadn't the week before.

She laid on the horn then shouted at the driver who had just cut her off, showing a tiny glimpse of the bad girl she had let out once and only once in her twenty-six years and didn't dare let out again. She justified the brief transgression by pointing out the other driver couldn't hear her through the windows of her '67 rag-top Mustang, closed against the late January chill of Albuquerque, New Mexico. Of course, it didn't help that she hadn't had a man in her life for...well, much longer than she cared to think about. Especially when Valentine's Day loomed around the corner and every-where she turned red and pink hearts were popping out at her, reminding her of the pathetic state of her love life.

She glanced at her watch. What also didn't help was that she'd been waylaid by an accident on I-40, and now grumpy and preoccupied Monday morning drivers threatened to send her careening over an emotional edge that she'd preferred not to be teetering on just then.

"Marie Antonia Bertelli, is that the mouth you use to talk to your mother?"

Marie sighed and moved her wireless phone from under her chin where she'd thought her mother couldn't hear her. Ha. "I wasn't talking to you, Mama."

Although for all intents and purposes she should say exactly what she'd said to the driver to Francesca Bertelli. Her mother sometimes acted like she'd immigrated from Italy last week, with her old-world traditions and speech patterns, rather than the second generation Italian-American that she was, who'd placed first runner-up in the Miss New Mexico beauty pageant.

Francesca went on as if they hadn't been interrupted. "About dinner tonight. I want you to wear the blue dress. You know the one I'm talking about? The one you wore to Anthony's wedding. It makes you look like you have breasts. And, of course, it brings out the blue in your eyes."

Marie's mood worsened with each word her mother said. "I'm not coming to dinner tonight, Mama," she told her for the third time in as many minutes. Her mother had a habit of only hearing those things she chose to hear. Which was very little of what Marie had to say.

"The blue dress," her mother said again.

The blue dress was the most hideous of hideous bridesmaid's dresses and was packed away in the bottom of a box somewhere, though Marie had seriously considered burning it. The poofy clown-like nightmare made her look like a blue elephant.

"I'm making your favorite. Farsumagru o briolone. You have to come to dinner," her mother complained.

The Sicilian meat roll wasn't her favorite. It was her older brother Frankie Jr.'s favorite. But to tell her mother that now would only encourage her to go on. In fact, the mix-up might be a trap altogether. Entice her into an argument of what they would have for dinner, and she would end up going to the dinner and forgetting that it was the last thing she wanted to do tonight…or ever.

Marie bit the inside of her cheek. She'd finally moved into her own apartment a week ago after living with her family for ten months upon her return from L.A. Since the move, every morning like clockwork her mother called to invite her to dinner. Marie had made the mistake of going last Sunday, thinking there was only so much her mother could do during a family meal. She'd been sorely mistaken. There, seated to her right, had been Benito Benini, a guy she'd gone to kindergarten with and twenty years was not enough time to erase the memory of him launching green Play-Doh out of his nose. A nose that had grown considerably since then.

"No," Marie said. "Absolutely not." She hesitated as she negotiated a right-hand turn into the Bernalillo County Courthouse parking lot. "I…I already have plans."

She resisted the urge to bang her forehead against the steering wheel as she said the words. What was she thinking?

"Plans? With whom? What's his name? Do we know him?"

"We," of course, referred to the entire Bertelli family. Her father, Frank Sr. Her mother. And her three older brothers, Frankie Jr., Anthony and Mario, all married and either with or starting families of their own.

And each with their own reason for butting into every aspect of Marie's private life.

"Never mind, Mama," Marie said as she zoomed into a parking space in front of another car. She ignored the blast of the other driver's horn and gave a friendly wave. She moved the wireless phone to her other ear then shut off the car engine. "Look, I've got to go. I'm at the courthouse and I'm already late meeting my client."

"Late? See, you should have stayed home. You wouldn't be late if you were home."

"I was late because there was an accident, Mama. The highway was backed up for miles."

"Accident? You got into an accident?"

"No. I said there was an accident. One that, I am happy to say, I was not involved in." But with five minutes more of this conversation she might wish otherwise. "Goodbye, Mama. I'll call you later."

"This is how you would leave your mother? Worrying about what ax murderer you're meeting tonight?"

Marie leaned her head on the rest behind her. "I'm not going out with an ax murderer. I'm meeting Dulcy and Jena for dinner."

"Oh."

Was that a note of disappointment in her mother's voice? Yes, it definitely was. The realization made even her little white lie easier to swallow.

Marie smiled. Interesting. Was her mother to the point where she'd welcome even a potential ax murderer into the family just so long as he was a possible husband?

"You could bring them to dinner. It's been so long since we've seen your friends."

That was because on the few occasions that her best friends had met up with her family the police had almost needed to be brought in. Mostly because Jena had a hard time believing the family really did think they had a right to meddle in Marie's life and had challenged them on the point. And the Bertellis had a habit of referring to Jena as "the loose one" who would tarnish their only daughter's reputation.

If only that were the case. Marie couldn't even *pay* for a reputation, good, bad or otherwise.

"I don't think so, Ma. Gotta go. Love you, bye."

She clicked her wireless closed on her mother's automatic protest then quickly switched the phone off altogether, routing any incoming calls to her voice mail.

How she'd survived twenty-six years in the Bertelli family was anyone's guess. And the phone conversation she'd just had with her mother was nothing compared to what it was like to actually grow up in the Bertelli house. Directions on how she should do this, wear that, fix this. Oh, she adored her family. Loved them to death. Unfortunately, she also feared they would be the death of her.

She put her keys in her purse and gathered her things together from the passenger seat. Whatever had possessed her to pick up her phone without looking at the display so early in the morning? She should have known it would be her mother trying to railroad her into another blind date with another old classmate that used to do something disgusting with play materials. Last week it had been third grade and Johnny Russo who had tried to paste her to her desk chair. The week before that she'd been hopeful that her family was running out of prospects when they'd actually invited a third cousin to dinner. A cousin was family, no matter how many times removed, and she'd easily sidestepped that matchmaking attempt by casually bringing up the increase in risk of birth defects all throughout dinner. "Why just the other day I heard that someone who had married her cousin four times removed on her mother's side had a baby with two noses. *Two.*" She'd held up two fingers to emphasize her point.

Marie hoisted her bulging briefcase from the passenger's seat, wondering if coming up with inventive stories to shock her parents was going to be the state of her life forever or if eventually her family would wake up and realize that what *they* had in mind for her, and how *she* saw her life, were two completely different things. She didn't want to be matched up with a guy to whom marriage was synonymous with slavery. Didn't want a loveless marriage to a man who was acceptable by the sole criteria that he was either full-blooded Italian or Italian-American and knew the difference between pinzimonio and agliata.

You would have thought they'd have learned after she ran away to L.A. nearly three years ago.

Marie stared at her reflection in the rearview mirror, scrunching a couple of runaway red curls, then smoothing the liner under her right eye. No, she supposed her family wasn't very quick on the uptake. When they'd virtually gone ahead and planned a wedding without her being aware of it, sent out invitations and the whole nine yards, then told her a week before the event that she was marrying a man coming in from Italy, she'd finally blown her stack and pointed her vintage '67 Mustang in the direction of L.A. and hadn't stopped until she got there. Not even her best friends, Dulcy and Jena, had known where she was until she'd landed a job in the L.A. district attorney's office and had sublet an apartment from a B-movie actress going off on a two-month film shoot in South America. She'd passed onto them the responsibility of telling her family she was okay. She hadn't been surprised to find out they'd filed a missing person's report on her. She'd spent two hours on the phone with the Albuquerque sheriff's office assuring them she was fine and wasn't rotting away in a Dumpster somewhere.

She hadn't directly contacted her parents until three weeks after that. She'd called and told them she was okay, that she hoped the wedding went well without her, and that she would be in touch. Nothing more. Because she knew if she had told them where she was, her brothers would have promptly been sent to drag her back home.

No, she hadn't shared her apartment address until she was sure her parents had gotten the picture. Either butt out of her personal life or she was going to butt out of their lives…permanently.

Of course, that really hadn't been her first real revolt. The first one had involved sexy neighbor Ian Kilborn, a lifetime of suppressed hormones, and a boatload of rebellion aimed toward her controlling family. But only she, Ian and the pantry walls knew about that one incident—a steamy, heat-filled white-hot flash in time when she was eighteen and had unleashed the wild woman that lurked just below her good-girl surface. And, oh, what a time she and naughty Ian had had. And if now, eight years later, she thought about reliving the event every now and again, it was only because, instead of living down the street from each other, she and Ian now spent most of their time in the same courthouse as attorneys.

Marie self-consciously cleared her throat as she

climbed from the car, then closed the door after her. January in Albuquerque, New Mexico, was a world away from the weather L.A. was experiencing right now. And she'd still be there enjoying the sun and her freedom if Dulcy and Jena hadn't contacted her nearly a year ago and held her to the promise they'd made when they were young. They'd convinced her to sign on with well-known attorney Bartholomew Lomax and establish the partnership they'd always planned on.

And now her mother was resorting to her old behavior.

A hot guy exited the seven-story brand-spanking-new courthouse as she neared. Marie smiled at him but he seemed to see right through her. He passed and she slowed her step. Was she really that desperate that she had to rely on her family to fix her up to land a man? She glanced at her plain navy-blue suit. Okay, so maybe she wasn't Nicole Kidman, and she was on the short side, but she'd never thought she was unattractive.

Was she?

A man opened the courthouse door in front of her. She moved to step around him only he entered before her, nearly causing her to slam into his back. She frowned then caught the door before it could slam against her back.

Okay…

So maybe she was having a bad day. Everyone had them every now and again, didn't they?

If only it didn't look like she was having a bad decade.

She hurried down the hall, trying to forget the state of her personal life and concentrate on her professional—something she usually did very well.

"Marie!"

She was halfway down the hall before she realized someone was calling her name. She turned to find her friend and partner Jena McCade rushing after her.

"God, woman, where is your head? I must have called you three times before you heard me."

Marie made a face. Jena looked great. As usual. With her shiny straight black hair, her sexy figure, her confident posture, Marie was sure no one ever let a door close on Jena.

Of course, now that Jena was married to ex-hockey hunk Tommy "Wild Man" Brodie, her attractiveness seemed to have merely increased. Her skin always seemed flushed and her eyes always had a faraway dreamy look in them. Jena had told Marie and Dulcy that it was the properly laid look. Marie preferred to think it was love.

Jena twisted her lips. "I'd ask if it was a man messing with your head, but I'm guessing it's probably your mother."

"Right." Marie made a face. "She wants me to come to dinner again tonight." She looked down at the hall. "What are you doing down here so early?"

"Judge Bullock wanted to talk to me in chambers. Seems there have been some problems with the district attorney's office and all cases are being put on hold."

"Oh?"

Jena waved her hand and continued walking down the hall, forcing Marie to turn to face her. "Shouldn't impact your big corporate case. Something to do with new DNA procedures."

"Good. I'd just as soon have this case over with as not."

"Difficult run?"

"No. Just boring."

Jena laughed. "That's the first time I've heard you say that."

"This is the first time I've ever felt this way."

"You know, your mother wouldn't get to you so much if you weren't so picky about men yourself," Jena said.

Marie made a strangled sound.

"What?"

"I can't believe you just said that." Marie glanced around the hall. Another attorney she was vaguely familiar with grinned as he moved past them. "And in front of so many other people."

Jena crossed to stand in front of her. "I can't believe you haven't gotten laid in over a year." She poked her perfectly manicured finger against Marie's blue suit jacket. "And you pay entirely too much attention to what other people think."

"I'm not picky."

Jena smiled. "Yes, you are. Why else aren't you dating anyone?"

"Because I've been busy helping get a law practice going."

"So have Dulcy and I, but that hasn't stopped us."

If Marie thought her day was bad before, it had very definitely just taken a deep nosedive.

Jena started walking backward toward the door. "Take my advice, Marie. The next guy you see? Grab him and don't let him go until he wipes that ever-present grimace from your face."

"I don't grimace."

Jena began to turn around, the distance between them lengthening. "I'll see you back at the office later then?"

"Office. Yeah."

Marie stood for long a moment staring after her friend's retreating back. Oh, sure, to be Jena's friend was to be in a perpetual state of mortification. If Jena wasn't sharing details on her orgasms and the frequency of them, she was commenting in a very open way about others' sex lives.

Marie just wished Jena hadn't picked that moment to aim a very sharp arrow at Marie's sex life.

She absently raised her fingers to her lips. Did she grimace? She suddenly realized that, yes, she did. Quite frequently. In fact, she couldn't remember the last time she'd smiled. Really smiled. Was it a week ago? A month?

What was she thinking? Of course she smiled. She smiled all the time. Just this morning she'd smiled at the guy at the coffee shop. Hadn't she?

She directed a frustrated wave down the hall to dismiss her friend and her unwelcome advice. Of course, Jena was right in that it had been awhile since she'd dated. Heck, she'd even caught herself eyeing Play-Doh nose's powerful thighs last week for a brief second. The moment of insanity had, of course, been followed quickly by the overpowering urge to vomit.

Grab the next man she met, indeed...

She turned the corner and ran smack dab into the last man she should grab. But she'd be damned if she didn't want to grab him anyway.

ONE MINUTE, IAN KILBORN had been thinking about the perfectly good proposition the pretty court reporter had just thrown his way. The next, he was running into the woman he'd spent a good portion of his adult life thinking about having sex with again without a chance in hell of its coming to pass.

Ian caught Marie Bertelli by the arms and stared down into her flushed face. At one time a quirky eye-catching little girl down the street, now she was a sexy-as-all-get-out full-grown woman. It didn't seem to matter that years had passed since anything intimate had passed between them, or that they were both attorneys now, or that he'd had countless women since Marie. No matter what else was going on in his life, he'd inevitably find his thoughts beginning and ending with the good girl/wild child that had crawled under his skin a long time ago and he had never been able to rid himself of.

Ian's gaze skimmed her features. Damn, but she was stunning as hell up this close and personal. And that she had no idea just how sexy she was only lent to her appeal. But what got to him was that no matter how much time passed, the thundering desire that ignited in him for the fiery redhead was still immediate, complete, and more than a tad uncomfortable. Red-hot memories of cramped spaces and soft moans and great sex made him one very horny adult for this woman he'd always had the hots for, and probably always would.

"You can let go now."

While he watched the words exit Marie's provocative little mouth, it took a moment for them to register in Ian's brain.

He cocked a grin at her. "Are you sure? Looks to me like you still need a little propping up."

The color in her cheeks deepened as she batted at his hands, nearly dropping her briefcase in the process. She glanced around, only there was no one around to witness their collision. While the main corridor was always busy, the side halls were usually pretty quiet, allowing for a privacy Ian hadn't had with Marie for nearly eight years. And his body was letting him know that it had been much too long.

He chuckled quietly as he let her go, mildly amused by her fussing with her suit.

She blew out a long, shaky breath. "God, will you ever change, Ian Kilborn? I swear, when you wake up in the morning, the first thing on your mind must be sex. And it's probably the last thing you think about every night before going to bed…"

He scanned her features, only half hearing what she was saying. He'd learned a long time ago about that if you wanted to hear what Marie had to say, you didn't listen to her words, but rather her body language. And the shaky breath she'd just exhaled, the way she slowly smoothed her free hand over her hip, and the quiet tone of her voice combined to tell him that not much had changed since their tryst in her parents' pantry. He had the feeling that, if he asked, she'd hand him her panties right there and then. And, oh, how tempting it was to do just that.

He grimaced. Of course this fortuitous meeting would have to come on the heels of the phone call he'd received from her father yesterday. And for that reason alone the last thing on his mind right now, or at any time in the immediate future, should be Marie's panties.

It dawned on him that she had stopped speaking. He tugged his gaze away from the way her jacket draped over her soft breasts then blinked up into her eyes.

And he froze.

There, in the depths of her blue, blue eyes, lurked a curious and suspicious determination.

Ian squinted at her. Uh-oh. He knew that look only too well. She'd worn it only one other time. And while that one other time had led to his finally stroking her sweet, slick flesh, it had also held the potential for disaster if her family found out what had gone on in the tiny room off the kitchen.

An aroused Marie was a breathtaking sight. A rebellious Marie scared the living hell out of him, no matter how much he wished they were back in that pantry right then.

Ian smoothed down his tie to keep from reaching out and touching her, then cleared his throat.

But Marie spoke first. "You have a case this morning?"

Ian raised his brows at her softly spoken words. "Filing a motion."

She smiled at that. "The caped crusader for criminals is hard at work, huh?"

He took a physical step backward. "Something like that."

When was the last time he'd seen her aside from down the hall of the courthouse? Three months? No, two. Judge Bullock's Christmas party. She'd been friendly then as well. But he suspected it was because she'd been as sorry to be at the party as he had been and was grateful for a familiar face. He'd spent a few minutes talking to her about the weather, noting how she'd scratched at her dress as if she couldn't stand the material against her skin.

And what a dress and skin it had been, too. Marie had always leaned toward the conservative side. High-neck blouses, loose-fitting jackets and longer skirts. But that night she'd had on a sexy number that fit her in more ways than one. And he'd been hard-pressed not to follow her around the party, tongue panting, in the hope that she'd take pity on him and bring him home with her.

Now he looked at her and wondered if she'd somehow found out about her father having secretly retained his services. But no. He didn't think Marie had that type of self-control. When she found out, and he was sure she would, she wouldn't be quite this...nice.

"You know, I was just thinking," she said now, jarring him out his thoughts. "Ever since you moved back here from Chicago, we really haven't had a chance to talk, have we?" She licked her lips, a move he suspected was completely unconscious, which made it all the more mesmerizing. "You know, caught up on things." She shifted her briefcase from one hand to the other. "What are you doing tonight?"

2

NOW THAT WAS A LOADED question, wasn't it?

Marie stared up into Ian's strikingly handsome, fear-stricken face and wondered why she didn't just come out and ask him if he was up for Round Three in the Marie and Ian physical relationship match. Of course in terms of sex it would only be Round Two, but she always rated the first time they'd kissed as Round One simply because it was the first time she'd ever climaxed.

She fought to keep her gaze straight. And that's exactly what she wanted now, wasn't it? For him to give her another out-of-this-world orgasm? To exorcise the rebellious emotions roiling through her bloodstream? To have sex? Wild, decadent, monkey sex with the man most qualified for the job?

Just think, an orgasm and revenge in one fell swoop...

Marie gulped, thinking she'd finally careened over the edge.

Insane. Unthinkable. Absolutely impossible.

And tempting.

Naughty Ian Kilborn was ten times more charming now than he'd ever been, making the prospect of sleeping with him even more appealing. But that wasn't why she was thinking what she was. He was the ultimate way to get her family back for interfering in her life yet again.

The only problem was having sex with Ian wasn't nearly as simple as all that and she needed a few minutes to remind herself why.

But then she remembered she was already running late and that she really didn't have time for this, and damn Jena and her sex-fiendish ideas anyway. "Never mind—"

"I already have plans," Ian said at the same time.

Well, that really stank, didn't it? Before she could retract her loaded question, he'd turned her down cold.

Marie absently wondered how the planets were aligned and just which one of them had it in for her this morning.

"Well, then," she said, trying to shrug off the uncomfortable sensation sticking to her skin along with the sizzling heat produced just by being close to Ian, "I guess I'll see you around the courthouse."

"How about tomorrow night?"

Marie stared at him, her nipples bunching into tight points. "I already have plans," she lied.

His grimace could match, if not better, any of hers. "There's something I think you and I need to discuss."

That got a suggestive smile out of her. "Oh? And would that conversation include words?"

His eyes held the onset of one of his killer grins.

"I've got to get going," she said and rounded him. She also needed to have her head examined. What was she thinking, leading Ian Kilborn to believe she was interested in anything more than throwing darts at his picture on her wall? No matter how much her body vibrated like a divining rod whenever he was within a hundred feet of her?

She purposely kept her back straight as she hurried down the hall. Okay, so maybe she didn't really have his picture on her wall. Well, not now, anyway. But she had at one point. She'd used her father's copy machine to blow up Ian's senior class picture and had hung it under a poster of Shawn Cassidy inside her closet door. Whenever she'd had a bad day, she'd take Shawn down and have at it with the darts she'd swiped from her brothers' dartboard in the garage.

Of course, the look on her mother's face when they'd painted her room later that year and all the holes in her closet door had been revealed was absolutely priceless. Marie had told her they must have termites. Her mother called in the exterminators the next day.

Marie finally rounded the corner, then leaned against the wall out of sight of Ian. She didn't check to see if he'd watched her depart because she was afraid of her reaction if he hadn't.

"Miss Bertelli. I was afraid you weren't going to make it."

Marie nearly jumped out of her skin as a young man addressed her.

She drew in a deep breath and tried for a smile for her client, the owner of a small computer programming company being sued for copyright infringement.

Business. All business. That was going to be Marie Bertelli for the rest of the day.

And if she was just a wee bit afraid that might be the inscription on her gravestone…well, she wasn't going to go there now.

IF IAN KILBORN NEEDED A reminder of just how small the world really was, running into Marie Bertelli was exactly the stimulus. It was midafternoon but he felt like he was still standing in the courthouse hall watching her walk away from him. Puzzlement, interest, and a deep burning sensation combined to completely distract him.

Thirteen years since they'd met and he still couldn't figure out what, exactly, the attraction was. But, oh boy, was there ever one. He'd been seventeen, she'd been thirteen, and one little blink of her blue eyes had rendered him little more than putty in her hands right from the start. And while he held off stripping her of her virginity until she was eighteen, it still took little more than a blink to get him hot and bothered all over again.

Only he'd never let her know that. He scratched the top of his head, then smoothed his hair back in place. The reasons for keeping her in the dark had varied over the years. From the ridiculous adolescent excuse of never letting anyone know they had power over you, to the irrational adult fear of rejection that was crazy but very real just the same.

There had only been a brief two-year stretch when she'd been banished to the back of his mind and then only for geographical reasons. Chicago was a long way from Albuquerque, and further still from L.A. Yet that hadn't stopped him from having the occasional white-hot dream about her, or catching a glimpse of a woman and thinking it might be her even though she was at least thirteen hundred miles away.

Sex, pure and simple. That's what he'd told himself then, and that's what he continued to tell himself now. There was something exciting and unforgettable about forbidden desire. About wanting something you knew you shouldn't and going after it anyway. She'd been thirteen and the youngest daughter of a family renowned for getting physical with the guys chasing after her if they didn't take the first verbal hint. But that hadn't stopped him from thoroughly kissing her—and wanting to go much further. But five years later at her brother's college graduation party, he'd done just that in her parents' pantry of all places.

Then there was his own Irish-Catholic family and their twisted ideas on procreation and how it should only be done with another Irish-Catholic.

Ian leaned back in his chair and grinned, thinking about how very small the world was. And as he glanced at some papers on his desk, he knew he had a very good reason to think that way.

He'd been careful about his attraction to Marie and had been spared not only the scrutiny of his own family, but the verbal and, thus, the physical reminders that little Marie Bertelli was off-limits to everyone except whoever her family approved of. Which was nobody in the neighborhood where they both lived. And, he suspected, nobody in the world—especially since he'd heard the story of what went down nearly three years ago with the groom from Italy.

It was shortly after Marie's taking off for L.A. that he'd accepted a job offer from a college friend in Chicago.

A high-profile case sat on the corner of his desk. Ian eyed the file, glanced at his watch, then at his calendar.

Ah, a very small world, indeed.

And Marie was about to find out just how small.

AT LEAST SHE WASN'T wearing the blue poofy dress.

Marie considered the very sad state of her life as she got out of her Mustang in the sweeping driveway of her parents' house. The two-story white stucco looked like it could have been at home in the Mediterranean or the southwest and stood a testament to large family life. This was where Marie had grown up. And the place she still called home even if she couldn't live there anymore.

It wasn't difficult to figure out what she was doing here. She'd gone straight home to her apartment after calling it a day to find the refrigerator she'd bought secondhand on the fritz and what she had planned to make for dinner not fit for a bad date. Her mother had called just as she'd discovered that and waved insalata malfitana in her front of her hungry face, reminding her that not only had she not had dinner but that far-sumagru o briolone *was* her favorite, not Frankie Jr.'s.

Okay, so she was weak. The way she figured it, she was entitled to be a little soft just this once. Her day had gotten better after bumping into Ian, but only marginally. She needed a little bit of her mother's fussing and worrying if just to remind her that someone did care.

Her gaze slid down the block where the Kilborn house still stood, even though the Kilborns didn't live there anymore. A Mexican-American family lived there now. But that didn't stop Marie from remembering how she used to sit on the front porch and mentally will Ian to drive by in whatever shiny new sports car he had at the time.

Ever since seeing him that morning, the craving that had pretty much defined her adolescence had anchored itself in her stomach, making her feel needy and hot and just a tad reckless.

Reckless. If she knew what was good for her, she'd completely forget the definition of that word. Whenever her family pushed a little hard, she tended to rebel in very dramatic ways—in ways that made even her outrageous friend Jena look good. Her dad pushed her, she slept with Ian Kilborn.

Oh, boy.

That was so not why she was here. She'd come to try to shrug off unwanted emotions via a dinner session with her family. She didn't want Ian any more than he wanted her.

Oh, yeah? Try telling that to her hormones.

She heard a long, wistful sigh and realized it was her own.

Oh, great. Grimacing and sighing. She was turning into a regular hopeless wonder.

Pulling her jacket closed against the late January chill, she stepped up the winding walkway to the door, briefly knocked, then let herself in. She told herself she knocked because she didn't want to find one or the other of her parents flagrante delicto. When she was twenty-one, she'd come home early from a party Jena had thrown. Marie shuddered at the memory of her parents going at it like randy teenagers on the foyer couch. Her mother often reminded her that it had only happened once and wasn't likely to happen again. But Marie wasn't taking any chances.

She peeked around the door then called out. Her mother's voice immediately responded from the kitchen, telling her to come in.

Marie shrugged out of her jacket, then hung it up in the closet. The sweet scent of basil filled the hall, leading her back to the kitchen. She couldn't remember a time when the house hadn't smelled like one spice or another mixed with the pungent scent of tomato. And when her mother made bread...

She gave a mental groan as she pushed open the

swinging door and moved into the airy, terra-cotta-tiled kitchen with its hanging copper pots and pans, pots of fresh herbs, strings of garlic and a table large enough to hold the entire Bertelli family, including her brothers' wives.

"You didn't wear the dress."

Marie made a face. How was it her mother could tell what she was wearing without even looking? "I didn't feel like wearing a dress."

Francesca Bertelli was well into her fifties but the image she portrayed was that of a much younger woman, despite the strands of silver in her thick red hair. Marie rounded the cooking island to where her mother was cleaning Spanish onions in the sink and kissed her cheek. "And you consider jeans and a sweatshirt proper attire?"

"For dinner at my parents?" She smiled. "Yes."

Her mother made her trademark sound of disapproval deep in her throat, even though her blue eyes shone with love and amusement.

"Where's Dad?"

Francesca motioned with the knife. "In his office. He'll be out in a minute."

Marie reached for a piece of mozzarella, then instead took a piece of cut celery on the counter.

"Eat the cheese. You're too skinny."

A familiar refrain. And a refrain that Marie had long since grown used to ignoring.

She automatically went to the cupboard to the right and reached for the plates.

"What are you doing?" her mother asked.

"Setting the table."

"It's set."

Marie squinted, wondering if her mother had inhaled

too many onion fumes as she stared at the clear kitchen table.

"We're eating in the dining room tonight."

Marie's hands froze where she still touched the plates. The dining room had been the one room in the house that should have been fully capitalized. THE DINING ROOM. The only room off-limits to her and her brothers when they were younger, and a room that was used only on holidays. She slowly withdrew her hands and closed the cupboard door. Sure, while Valentine's Day might be around the corner, the minor observance didn't rate on THE DINING ROOM scale.

"Mama…" she said in warning.

The last thing she needed was another unsuitable suitor to ruin a perfectly good dinner. She sighed and leaned against the counter. She'd assumed that since she'd been so late in accepting the dinner invitation that she wouldn't have to face another one of her mother's matchmaking attempts tonight.

She rubbed her throbbing temple. Knowing her mother, she'd probably made the trip across town to sabotage her daughter's refrigerator.

"Get the wine from over there on the counter and open it so it can air."

Marie turned and stared at the three bottles. She glanced back at her mother. "How many?"

"All of them."

Uh-oh. Her mother had given up on the one-by-one approach and was going to fill the table with possible grooms from hell.

She groaned, leaving the bottles right where they were. "You know, I'm suddenly not very hungry," she said, giving her mother a quick kiss on the cheek. "I'm going to go home.'' She swiped one of the mozzarella sticks. ''Tell Papa I said hi, won't you?''

She made a beeline for the kitchen door and the hall beyond, hoping to duck out of the house before the guests of honor arrived.

She swung open the door and, for the second time that day, ran straight into the hard, broad chest of Ian Kilborn.

IAN'S PHYSICAL RESPONSE to having Marie flush up against him for the second time that day was swift and unforgiving.

''We, um, have to stop bumping into each other this way,'' he said, surprised that his voice was low and gravelly.

Marie stared at him as if he'd grown another head. Well, he hadn't actually grown one, but one was growing just beneath the material of his slacks.

She leapt back and he quickly closed his suit jacket to cover any telltale bulges.

Only both he and Marie knew the truth.

''I didn't hear you come in,'' Marie's father said from where he stood behind Ian. ''Hello, baby girl.''

Marie's gaze shifted and so did the look in them as she skirted around him and gave her father a loud kiss on the cheek. ''Hi, Papa. I just got here.'' She cleared her throat as Frank Bertelli Sr. hugged her in his meaty arms, then released her. ''Unfortunately I, um, can't stay though.''

''Shame,'' Ian said.

Frankie and Marie both stared at him.

Okay, so maybe he could have been a little subtler. But the truth was that he didn't exactly intend for Marie to find out how really small the world was until some point down the road. Like maybe never.

"What's this nonsense? Of course you're going to stay," Frankie said, easily wrapping his arm around his daughter's shoulders, and then Ian's, and maneuvering them both through the kitchen door. "Your mama made your favorite."

Marie made a move Ian admired and wished he could emulate as she ducked right out of her father's grasp. "I know, I know. But the truth is I'm not feeling very well right now."

Ian eyed her. Sure, her color was high and her eyes overly bright. But he'd bet dollars to doughnuts that her physical state had nothing to do with any sort of illness. Rather her reaction was more likely due to the stimulus behind his own uncomfortable response: feeling her against him.

Frankie finally released him and Ian moved off to the side of the room, watching as Marie's mother swooped down on her, making a ceremony out of laying her hand against her forehead and cheeks checking for a temperature. Ian hid his smile and shoved his hands in his pockets. Oh, Marie's temperature had risen all right. But a fever wasn't to blame.

Ian knew what it was like to be the baby of the family. Much fussing and cooing and clucking had gone on in his house while growing up.

He also knew what it felt like to want something he knew he shouldn't have.

He moved the back of his collar away from his neck, finding his skin more than a little hot. To think, he'd gone thirteen years without letting the Bertellis in on how he really felt about their daughter. Now, after an accidental meeting or two he was a hairbreadth away from giving it all away.

Damn, she was beautiful. Even in her old sweatshirt and jeans, Marie Bertelli made him want to…well, get her out of that sweatshirt and jeans.

"I'm fine, Mama," Marie said, swatting Francesca's hands away from her face. "Just a little tired, that's all."

"You wouldn't be tired if you were staying in the house. Late nights, parties, dates with ax murderers. Lord only knows what's behind your not getting enough sleep."

"I get plenty of sleep." Ian watched her walk to the counter and pick up a bottle of red wine. "I've just been feeling a little stressed lately."

Ian watched her face blanch, as if she'd just said something she hadn't meant to. She popped the cork on the bottle of wine, then poured a healthy portion into a water glass.

"Stressed. Stressed. Of course you're stressed. Having to worry about keeping a house all by yourself." Her mother took the water glass, then poured the wine into a goblet without missing a beat.

Marie rolled her eyes and stared at Ian. He grinned. "It's an apartment, Mama, and… Oh, never mind." She swiped the wineglass and took a deep gulp from it. When she finished, her lips were a provocative shade of red, contrasting against the pinkness of her tongue as it flicked out to lick the corner of her mouth.

She narrowed her gaze on him. "What is he doing here anyway?"

Ian raised his brows. It had been awhile since someone had talked about him in the third person while he was still in the room.

And this particular room had just grown very, very quiet.

For a big man, Frankie Sr. could pull off uncomfortable remarkably well. And given Francesca's avoidance maneuvers as she returned to preparing dinner, Ian got the impression that she knew exactly what was going on.

The only person who didn't know was Marie.

And Ian knew she wasn't going to be very happy about it.

Frank cleared his throat. "Marie, I want to tell you the real reason I wanted you here tonight."

Ian stared at the older Italian. Frank had told him that he'd wanted to meet briefly. Hell, dinner hadn't even been mentioned, much less Marie's possible presence.

Not that it mattered, Ian reminded himself. Frank had no idea about Ian's past with his daughter.

"You've got to be kidding," Marie said dryly.

Ian glanced at her. Could he have been wrong? Did she already know?

"Marie," Frank said again. "I've hired Ian on to act as my attorney."

Where Marie's face had been filled with color only a moment before, it was now paper white. She blinked several times as if trying to absorb the words, to make sense out of them.

Obviously she hadn't known—not only about her father hiring Ian on, but about the trouble he was in.

Oh, boy.

And if things weren't complicated enough, Ian was afraid that if he and Marie were forced to be in the same room for any extended period of time, he was going to sleep with her.

Again.

Well, okay. Maybe that part wasn't so bad....

3

THE FOLLOWING MORNING Marie paced the waiting room outside Ian's office, hearing an odd sort of ticking in her head. Either somewhere in the high-tech offices of McCreary, Lopez and Daniels, Attorneys, there was a loud timepiece, or her own internal clock was counting off the seconds. And, no, it wasn't her biological clock. She didn't believe in such things. She had no real craving for children. At least not yet, anyway. Besides, at twenty-six, her biological time clock, if she did have one, hadn't even kicked on yet.

Had it?

Marie stopped in front of the receptionist's desk. "Is there a clock around here somewhere?"

The young blonde wearing slim black headphones blinked at her. "It's just after ten."

Marie stared at her.

"More precisely, two minutes after ten," the receptionist said, glancing at her watch.

Marie rolled her eyes. "That's not what I meant." She waved her hand and resumed pacing. "Oh, never mind."

Okay, so last night the last person she expected to run into at her parents' was Ian Kilborn. That alone would be enough to knock someone a little off-kilter. But she'd also run into him earlier that day and felt some peculiar yearnings she had thought she had locked up tight. As a result, her hormones had shifted into overdrive, reminding her that it had been a good long while since she'd played footsy with anyone between the sheets.

Then to find out that her father had Ian and his firm on retainer...

Tick tock, tick tock.

Marie squeezed her eyes shut, trying to halt the internal countdown, afraid of what would happen when the hand counted down to one.

Her mother...well, her mother had basically played her mother throughout dinner, telling Ian that the antipasto wasn't dinner when he reached for a second helping, sharing stories about Frankie Jr.'s exploits, and generally urging the conversation in every direction except in the one Marie wanted it to go.

Oh, sure, she'd casually tried to bring the conversation back around to Ian, his presence and his being her father's attorney. At least every two minutes. And every time she did she got three deadpan expressions and absolutely no words. At least until her mother came up with some other strange little tidbit to derail Marie's intentions.

Of course, it didn't help matters that she and Ian were essentially professional rivals and that her father's choosing to turn to him over her rankled something terrible. She felt something well beyond disappointment that her father couldn't see her as anything more than his daughter.

Marie made a low sound of frustration, earning her the receptionist's attention...again.

Marie stared back at her. "How long did you say Mr. Kilborn would be?"

The young woman looked down at her console then

pushed a button, speaking so quietly Marie couldn't make out her words.

Great. She was probably calling security.

"Marie."

Ian said her name like she was a long-lost friend just dropping in for a visit. A good friend. A friend he might be interested in being a little more…friendly with.

Marie turned to where he stood behind her, then squinted at him as if he'd lost his marbles when she knew perfectly well it was her own marbles that were in question.

Ian cleared his throat, thanked the suspicious receptionist, then motioned toward the doorway behind him. "What's say we go to my office."

"Mmm." Marie brushed past him, trying to ignore how good he looked, how in command, and how utterly sexy. She had no idea where his office was, but anyplace where she could speak to him in private was a good place in her book.

Well, okay, anyplace large enough so that she wouldn't have to smell the enticing scent of his skin and the subtle aroma of his cologne that reminded her of Albuquerque during the summer.

"Here," he said.

She entered the first office to the left that Ian indicated, then stopped in front of a wide glass-topped desk with thick iron legs. Ian rounded the table, smoothing his tie down, and looking altogether too yummy when all Marie wanted to do was scream.

"What a surprise," Ian said.

Surprise? There was absolutely nothing surprising about her being here. "Come on, Ian, admit it. You expected this visit.'' Marie pointed a finger at him. ''In fact, you're probably wondering why I'm so late.''

Ian's black eyes held amusement and warned of the coming grin. Marie braced herself. Ian toying with her she could handle. Ian and a genuine grin made her wish she hadn't put on panties this morning.

''I didn't know last night was going to go down the way it did,'' he said, motioning for her to sit.

She remained standing.

He sat.

As she suspected, she could see everything through the clear glass. The long bulk of his thighs. The way the fabric of his pants bunched at the crotch, hinting at what she already knew hid underneath.

Her throat grew tight.

''So why *are* you so late?''

Marie lifted her gaze to his grinning face, then made a face of her own that had nothing to do with a grin and everything to do with the grimace Jena accused her of wearing all the time.

But if ever there was a time to grimace…

''I had an evidentiary hearing at eight. I couldn't get here any earlier,'' she said automatically, then wondered why she'd offered the information at all.

Ian leaned back in the modern black leather and chrome chair and laced his hands together over his impossibly flat abdomen. ''I figured it would take that or an act of God to keep you from showing up here first thing.''

''Yes, well, if you hadn't run out of my parents' house in the middle of dessert last night I might have gotten some answers then.'' Or if his home address had been listed in the phone book, but she wasn't about to tell him she had gone so far as to call 411 in hopes of finding out where he lived. What she would have done with his address was better left a mystery unsolved. More than likely she would have headed over there, not only revealing she didn't have a life beyond work and her family, but risking running into him with someone else.

She narrowed her eyes. Was he seeing someone? The prospect made the hair on her arms stand on end. Though why, she didn't even want to begin to guess.

Ian slowly shook his dark head. "Come on, Marie. It doesn't matter if I had spent the *night* at your parents' house. I wouldn't have broken attorney–client privilege. And I think you know that."

She leaned forward and rested her palms against the cool glass. "Attorney–client privilege my rear end, Ian. He's my father. Family doesn't count when it comes to something like this."

He casually shrugged. "Then ask your father."

She had. A dozen times. With no results.

It was bad enough her family chose to view her law degree as so much artwork on the wall, believing one day she would come to her senses and see that a woman's place was with a husband and kids. And forget that it was downright humiliating to find out that her father had hired Ian—Ian Kilborn, for God's sake—as his attorney. When she'd finally gotten her father alone, as he was walking her to the door last night, he had nearly patted her hair and told her not to worry her pretty little head about it.

Actually, he had done exactly that.

Ugh.

"Ian..." she said in warning.

"Marie?" he responded, looking innocent.

Only both of them knew that Ian Kilborn, either as

a barracudalike defense attorney or the mouth-watering young man who had seduced her, was far from innocent.

Which made her present situation all the more trying.

She heaved a gusty sigh, walked one way and stared at the Chinese art on his wall, then the other and gazed at the black lacquer bookcase filled not with law books but crystal pieces, then stopped, tapping a finger against her lips. She wondered briefly how either of her friends would handle this situation.

Jena McCade-Brodie no doubt would round the desk, straddle his chair and seduce the information right out of him.

Dulcy Ferris-Landis would outwit every last detail from him without his being aware he'd said a word. Or, better yet, make it look like he'd offered up the information voluntarily.

Neither approach emerged appealing or likely in Marie's case. She didn't have Jena's oozing sexuality. And Dulcy...well, there was only one of her.

So Marie fell back on the next best thing.

"You know, Ian," she said, slowly turning back to face him. Oh, sure, he might have seduced her, but a girl didn't succumb to such talents without learning a thing or two. And since she'd done her share of thinking about the seduction she'd probably learned quite a bit. "There is, um, some interesting information that I might be able to share."

He must have caught on to the change in her demeanor because his chair snapped upright and his hands were no longer folded against his glorious abs. "I don't see that anything you'd have to say could help your father's case."

"No. No. You're right about that."

She took a wicked kind of pleasure watching the grin vanish from his handsome face.

Interesting that when he thought he was in control he looked like the cat that still held the mouse in his mouth. But now that she was threatening to turn the tables he looked more like the mouse. A devastatingly sexy mouse.

"However," she said, leaning her hands against his desktop again, although this time with a purposeful prowl that made him pull at his collar. She watched his gaze flick to the V in her blouse and she discreetly thrust out her breasts against the fabric. "There might be some information I could impart that my father might be interested in." She allowed her gaze to skim over his face. "In fact, I think what I have to say would interest my entire family."

"Your brothers?" Ian asked, seeming torn between looking down her blouse and concentrating on what she had just said.

"Uh-huh."

"You mean…"

Marie nodded. "That's exactly what I mean."

The battle was won as Ian's full attention focused on her face rather than her physical assets.

"You wouldn't," he said.

Marie couldn't help herself. She had to smile at that one. "Tell me, Ian…is that a risk you're willing to take?"

"Having your family find out about us? I mean, what happened between us?" He cleared his throat and this time when he smoothed his tie his movements were more concentrated. "No."

"I thought not." She stood to her full height, surprised to find her nipples tingling and her thighs very, very hot. "So tell me."

"YOUR FATHER'S UNDER investigation for racketeering. Well, more specifically, money laundering. But you get the idea."

Ian said the words clearly, carefully, then allowed Marie the time she needed to absorb the information.

Damn, she was beautiful. And sexy as all get out when she was upset. And she was definitely upset. Her eyes flashed. Her smooth skin flooded with color. And he could all but see the tips of her breasts pressing against the creamy silk of her shirt, even though she was no longer bending over his desk.

She might be dressed in her normal armor of crisp business suit, but if he wasn't mistaken, the skirt of this one was a little shorter, the blouse a little tighter. He wondered if she'd dressed with him in mind that morning. Then he threw the thought out when her deep intake of breath broke the silence.

"By whom?" she asked, all power trip gone from her expression, shock taking its place.

"The U.S. Treasury Department."

"The U.S. Treasury Department?" She finally took him up on his invitation and sat down. Well, she didn't so much sit down as collapse into the chair behind her.

"Yes, you know, they're going after him for tax evasion." Ian couldn't help it when his gaze flicked to where her knees showed below the hem of her skirt and her distracted state allowed a nice little peek at a tantalizing stretch of thigh and a flash of her white panties before she automatically crossed her legs.

"God, a scene from *The Untouchables* just flashed

through my mind,'' she whispered, her gaze focused somewhere out the window behind him.

Ian chuckled. While he was getting flashes of white panties, she was seeing old gangster films. ''Marie, we're not talking Eliot Ness here. Or Al Capone, for that matter.''

Her gaze settled on him, making him wish she were there for any other reason than what she was.

''Yes, but you know what they say about my family.''

''What? That because your father emigrated from Sicily when he was a teenager that he must be a member of the Cosa Nostra?''

She winced, reminding him of how hurt she used to be when the kids in the neighborhood teased her about her Italian heritage. Frank Sr. was secretly called Don Bertelli. Of course, not a one would dare say anything in front of her brothers, but there were plenty of times when Frankie Jr., Anthony and Mario weren't around. Many times, Ian had stepped in to take care of the situation without Marie or her family ever knowing about it.

She took a deep breath. ''My father owns a chain of dry cleaners, for God's sake. What could the Treasury Department possibly want from him?''

Ian rested his forearms against the desk he'd inherited from the guy who'd inhabited the office before him. The guy who had inherited the same office from the guy before him eight months before that. With that kind of track record, ever since his first day on the job, he'd considered his career to be on ice as thin as the glass of his table.

''That's what he hired me to find out.'' He pushed some papers out of his way. ''A treasury agent pulled him in the day before yesterday for some preliminary questioning.''

Marie's gaze finally seemed to focus on him. ''And he called you.''

Ian nodded. ''And he called me.''

She looked so sweetly and sexily confused that he had to force himself to remember this was the same woman who had just blackmailed him for the information he'd just shared.

He gave a frown. Of course, he never would have caved if he didn't have such a long history with Marie's family.

That had certainly been a factor in his accepting her father's case.

While he'd been blown away when his secretary had told him Frank Bertelli Sr. was on the phone for him two days ago, he'd been more than a little intrigued about why he was calling. And even more intrigued when Frank had asked him to come down and act as his attorney.

Why him? There had to be at least a hundred other attorneys he could have called. Why seek out the Irish kid that used to live in his neighborhood? Especially since he had a daughter who could handle his case just as easily.

Of course he hadn't asked either question, although he did still want to know the answers to them. No, instead he'd snatched up the case like he was still the little Irish kid down the block looking for a pat on the head when he'd done something right, like delivered the Bertelli Sunday morning paper on time.

Ian stretched his neck and discovered he'd been staring at the sexy curve of Marie's neck for a full minute, and that she had tuned into his interest and was looking at him with a mixture of curiosity and heat.

She licked her lips then quickly averted her gaze. "What evidence do they have?"

Ian shrugged. "I don't know yet. We're set up for a meeting with the agent in charge tomorrow afternoon."

She got to her feet, flashing him another view of her panties. Ian resisted the urge to pull at his too-tight collar again, suddenly thankful that Marie usually wore more concealing clothing. If he saw her panties again, he doubted he'd be able to stop himself from taking them off.

"I'm going to be there," Marie said.

"Be where?" Ian asked, distracted by his own thoughts.

"At the questioning, of course."

Ian got to his feet too, but the last thing on his mind was going anywhere near those panties. "Oh no, you're not."

Marie arched a brow at him.

"Come on, Marie. It's bad enough I told you what's going on. If you show up at that questioning, your father will know I told you."

"So?"

"So what's to say he isn't a bit upset by the news?"

She crossed her arms.

"Who's to say he won't fire my sorry ass and contact another attorney? You know, one that won't cave under the questionable tactics you just used to get me to talk. Then where will you be?"

And where would he be without this excuse to have Marie back in his life, even if for a little bit?

"Don't you mean where would *you* be?"

He squinted at her, wondering if she had been thinking the same thing he just had.

"Never mind. Forget I said that," she said.

Oh, how he wished he could. Because he had the sinking sensation that she hadn't been talking about his prospects for having sex with her again, but had instead been referring to her disapproval of his tendency to represent clients no one else would touch with a ten-foot pole.

And then there was her father…not exactly an ideal client either.

"Okay, okay," Marie derailed his train of thought. "So I don't go tomorrow." She rifled through her bag, then sighed when she apparently didn't find what she was looking for. "But I want you to tape the discussion for me."

"You want me to tape the questioning?" he enunciated.

She blinked at him. "Yes. Why?"

He slowly rounded the desk until he was standing directly in front of her. "Well, because I don't know how your father will react to my doing that."

Marie looked suddenly ill at ease. He watched her elegant throat work around a swallow. "My father…um, will do what you say because you're his attorney."

"And you?" he asked, halting mere inches away from her.

He always forgot about how petite she was until he was standing close to her this way. Marie's energy projected a much taller height than the five foot three that she was in her short heels. She was an intriguing mix of little girl and provocative woman. And right now he found himself wanting to get a glimpse again of those panties she had on.

"Ian?" she said half in question, half in warning.

"Hmm?"

He purposely allowed his gaze to travel leisurely over her tiny package. Oh, yeah, the ball had definitely just landed firmly in his court and he was going to hold on to it. Having Marie afraid of his next move, yet eager to see what it might be, was exactly the way he liked things between them. And while the last thing he should be thinking about was bedding his client's daughter, just then Marie wasn't Frank Sr.'s little girl, she was one-hundred-percent woman. More specifically, the woman he had seduced without really understanding why he'd done it beyond feeling the uncontrollable urge to do so.

And he was feeling that urge return to him tenfold.

"Ian?" Marie said more insistently.

Without even realizing he was doing so, Ian had backed her up until her bottom leaned against his glass desk. She held on to the blunted edge tightly with both hands and her small breasts moved with the sudden shortness of breath.

Ian realized he was having a little problem finding air himself. He eyed her mouth, but didn't kiss her. Instead he skimmed his hand down over her slender hip then slowly inched the material of her skirt up. She caught his hand, her eyes searching his, but her hand neither stopping nor helping him. He smiled at her then continued moving his hand until those white undies were revealed.

Oh, there was no thong for Marie Bertelli. Instead her underwear was cotton and white and sexier than any scrap of silk and lace known to man. It clung to her womanhood like only cotton could. And made his mouth water with the urge to lower himself to his knees and press his lips against the swollen flesh just underneath.

And one look into her eyes told him she wanted it just as much as he did.

A buzzing sound filled the room. While inwardly Ian jumped, outwardly he stood still as a statue, his hand burning from the feel of her upper thigh on his palm, and her fingers on the back of his hand.

"Don't you, um, think you should get that?" Marie asked, her voice barely above a whisper.

He could tell she was trying to play down her reaction, make him believe that his taking a peek at her underwear hadn't affected her one way or another. But Ian knew Marie sexually better than anyone else on Earth. And even if she had been able to control her voice, he would have known she wanted him.

"It's not mine," he said quietly.

Marie blinked once, then again. "My wireless," she said. Then her eyes widened. "My wireless! I'm waiting for a call telling me when the judge has reached his decision on my motion."

Ian hated to remove his hand. Really hated to have to let her go. But Marie gave him little choice as she wriggled away from him and his desk and reached for her purse and the cell phone inside. She turned away to take the call, leaving Ian staring after her like a dumbstruck teen who had just gotten his first look at a naked woman.

Only he hadn't seen naked. Not this time. He absently rubbed his chin as he listened to her speak. Actually, he'd never really gotten to see her naked. Not entirely. He'd seen her breasts. Caught glimpses of her tight bottom. But while he'd felt every inch of her, he'd never actually fully seen her.

And, in that one moment, he found he wanted that more than anything.

And knew that he wasn't going to get it.

Marie clapped her phone closed and backed toward the door. "The, um, judge has made her decision. I'm due back in court in fifteen."

Ian crossed his arms, doing what she had done minutes before—namely, trying to pretend he wasn't affected one way or another by the news.

And he knew he was as successful as she'd been at hiding his true state. "You'd better get running then."

Doubt and curiosity filled her eyes. "Yeah. I'd better get running."

Ian cleared his throat. "So...I'll see you tomorrow after the meeting?"

"The meeting? Oh, yes, the meeting." She glanced at her watch. "Why don't you give me a call when you're done? Maybe we can meet somewhere afterward."

"You don't want to come here?"

He realized how loaded that question was when she glanced at him, then his desk and back again. "Um, I don't think it's a good idea." She smiled at him. "Who knows what people might think?"

"Mmm," he agreed.

She turned toward the door, then appeared to change her mind at the last minute as she paused.

Then she rushed him.

Ian was rendered completely speechless as she pressed him against the desk, then molded her mouth against his. She made a small sound in her throat as her tongue darted out, first outlining his lips as if it was something she'd been wanting to do all day, then dipping it between his lips. He groaned and reached for her, but she quickly stepped away.

He stared at her as she straightened her skirt and exited his office, closing the door with a soft click behind her.

For long moments he stood there, the edge of his desk against the back of his legs, wondering just what in the hell had happened. And wondering just how he could go about making it happen again. Then telling himself he shouldn't let it happen at any point in the future, either near or far, if he had half a brain in his head.

He absently rubbed his chin.

Wow...

4

MONA LYNDELL BANGED THE carafe of coffee down onto the conference table, jolting Marie from her thoughts and nearly launching her straight from her chair.

Marie blinked at the firm's usually mild-mannered secretary, surprised that the movement hadn't been the accident she'd expected it to be. Rather the expression on Mona's face as she stared—or rather glared—at firm senior partner Barry Lomax was enough to turn the hot coffee into ice cubes.

"Uh-oh," Jena leaned closer to Marie and whispered. "Don't look now but I think we're witnessing a lovers' quarrel."

Marie's eyebrows hiked high on her forehead. Lovers' quarrel? What was Jena talking about? Mona had worked for Barry for nearly thirty years. Barry had been married three times, not once to his secretary. Her gaze moved from the couple in question, noting the way Mona appeared to seethe while Barry continued on outlining the partners' cases and who was handling what and who needed an assist in other cases.

Mona left the conference room seeming to take all the tension with her.

Marie crossed her arms and leaned back in her chair, wondering when the entire world had stopped making sense.

The roomy conference room at the firm of Lomax, Ferris, McCade and Bertelli was airy and decorated with a real feel for the Albuquerque American Indian culture, just like the offices and waiting area. Usually the surroundings relaxed her. But as she looked at Barry Lomax—Dulcy's mentor and friend who had invited the three of them to sign on with him to ensure his legal legacy when he retired—she suddenly felt like an entire subculture existed right under her nose without her knowing about it.

At the end of the table, Dulcy—five months pregnant and practically glowing with the happiness of her life— corrected Barry on one of her cases, while, next to Marie, Jena tapped her pen against her legal pad and glanced at her watch, no doubt anxious to get home to her ex-hockey player/doctor husband.

Truthfully, she hadn't been able to concentrate on a whole lot since leaving Ian's office earlier. And although three hours had passed since she'd planted a hot wet one on him, she swore she could still taste him on her lips.

She reached for the coffee with the intention of washing him off. But since chicken soup and a half of a sandwich at lunch hadn't succeeded, she doubted this would work either. She raised the steaming black liquid to her lips. Maybe she could scald the taste away.

Barry sighed and sat back in his chair. "I think we're done. Anyone have any new business to discuss?"

"Nope," Jena said, closing her notepad. "I think that about covers it."

"For me, too," Dulcy said.

Marie sat forward and leaned her forearms against the table. "Actually, I have something."

Three pairs of eyes focused on her, making her wish she hadn't said anything.

"Well, it's not something in the traditional sense of having something. It's not a new case or anything…"

Jena elbowed her. "Get to the point, Bertelli."

Marie grimaced at her and sighed. "I just thought that you all should know that the Treasury Department is questioning my father in connection with a racketeering charge."

Dead silence. Marie could virtually hear her own heart beating as she waited for some sort of verbal response. And waited. And waited.

She cleared her throat. "The details are a little sketchy yet," she said. "But I'm in contact with his attorney. Basically, all I know is that two days ago my father was pulled in for preliminary questioning at which time he contacted an attorney."

"Not you," Jena said quietly.

Marie looked down at the table where she was worrying her hands. She put her hands in her lap. "No."

At the end of the table, Dulcy shifted in her chair, not an easy move given her ever widening girth. "Who did he retain?"

"Ian Kilborn."

"Who?" Jena asked, leaning closer.

Marie stared at her. "Ian Kilborn."

Jena stared at her as if she'd gone soft in the head, then looked at Dulcy who gave an odd sort of smile before averting her gaze and pretending an interest in the files in front of her.

"Who's Ian Kilborn?" Barry asked.

Jena waved her hand. "We all grew up together in the same neighborhood. You wouldn't know him from there, of course, but you might be familiar with him by the cases he's represented lately.''

Dulcy nodded. ''There's Raphael Mendoza…''

''Serial robber who steals women's intimate apparel,'' Jena added.

Marie sank lower in her chair.

''That guy who killed his priest after he confessed to killing his wife,'' Dulcy counted off on her fingers.

''Jamieson.''

''Yeah, that's him.''

Jena lifted a finger. ''Then there's the Britney Hiawatha case.''

This lifted Barry's snow-white brows, making him look more like James Brolin than Sean Connery. ''The prostitute who…''

He didn't need to finish, because the story made news due to the sheer gruesomeness of the details. Hiawatha had basically turned any johns who didn't pay her into modern-day eunuchs.

And if Ian hadn't gotten his clients off altogether, he'd gotten the prosecutors to cop to lesser charges after pulling a few courtroom stunts that had nearly gotten him disbarred.

''Oh, he's good,'' Barry said, shaking his head. ''Very good. I'm surprised I didn't recognize the name. Kilborn, right? Kill 'em Kilborn.''

Marie rubbed her forehead. It was bad enough that this was the man her father had hired. This was also the guy she fantasized about sleeping with while… well, while she was sleeping and had no control over where her thoughts ventured.

Good Lord.

''You and Kilborn grew up together?'' Barry asked.

"In the same neighborhood," Marie said. "We weren't exactly...friends."

She caught Jena giving Dulcy one of those "really?" faces she hated and felt the urge to elbow her friend so hard she'd fall backward in her chair.

"Oh," Dulcy said.

But she hadn't said it in the way Marie might have expected. Instead, she seemed surprised by something that didn't have anything to do with the present conversation.

Marie looked at her. Dulcy's face had gone white and she was clutching her stomach.

"Are you all right?" Marie asked, getting up from her chair and hurrying toward her friend.

Then Dulcy smiled, so brightly it nearly hurt to look at her. "I'm...fine. I just felt the baby kick." She laughed. "I mean, at five months, I've felt him kick before, but not this insistently." She rubbed her palms over her stomach. "Ezzie jokes that I'm going to have a horse. I'm beginning to think she may be right."

Ezzie was Esmeralda, Dulcy and Quinn's housekeeper, although she was more family than hired help, especially since she didn't get paid. Marie got the heebies whenever she was around the old Indian woman because Ezzie looked at her as if trying to figure something out. Marie never stuck around long enough to find out what.

"That's why I'm never having children," Jena said, closing her notepad again. "I don't want any little hellion kicking around inside of me for nine months."

"They don't kick until after the first trimester," Dulcy corrected her.

Jena shrugged. "Six months, nine. Both too long."

Dulcy took Marie's hand and rested it against her

round belly. As she always did when she touched her friend's stomach, Marie wondered at how hard and solid the mass was. "Do you feel him?"

Marie did. She gasped and nearly drew her hand away at the force of the kick.

Barry chuckled as he got up and headed for the door. "I think that's my cue to leave the room."

Dulcy looked at him. "Don't you dare, Bartholomew. You get over here and feel your honorary grandchild along with everyone else."

Marie drew back from the group, watching as if from a distance. Her brother Frankie Jr.'s wife had had their two children while Marie was in L.A. Though she'd flown in for the births and the baptisms, she hadn't actually experienced the pregnancies with her sister-in-law. To watch one of her best friends go through the experience...well, she felt humbled and awed. And maybe, just maybe, a little envious.

"It's a girl," Jena said confidently after shaking her hand as if she'd just touched a bagful of goo instead of her friend's stomach. "I don't know why you don't want to find out what sex it is, Dulc. You keep calling it a 'he.' What if it is a girl?"

Dulcy gave a long, happy sigh. "I use 'he' just to keep things simple. Quinn and I would be very happy if it were a girl." She tucked her hair behind her ear and went through the maneuvers required for her to stand. "But Ezzie's adamant about my having a boy."

Marie shuddered. "That woman gives me the creeps."

"That's funny," Dulcy said, waving Barry away when he tried to help her get up. "She reminds me a lot of your grandmother."

Marie widened her eyes. So that's why she felt

strange around Ezzie. She realized with a start that her friend was right. Ezzie was exactly like Marie's Grandmother Maria, after whom she'd been named.

Yikes.

"So," Dulcy said, gathering her things from the table in front of her, "what happens with your father from here?"

Her father? Oh, her father.

"Um, he meets with the treasury agents tomorrow."

"Are you going?" Jena asked.

"No. But Ian's going to fill me in on everything."

"Mmm."

Marie glared at her friend. "Mmm, what?"

Jena shared another one of those looks with Dulcy. "Nothing. Did I say anything, Dulcy?"

"I didn't hear you say anything."

"Oh, piss off, the both of you."

All three of her friends and fellow attorneys stared at her as if she'd just dyed her hair bleach blonde. Marie instantly wanted to duck under the table until all of them forgot she had just said what she had—which would probably be never because she never swore. Even if the swear word ranked way over on the conservative side.

Barry held up his hands. "I'm out of here. See you guys tomorrow."

He left the room, leaving Marie behind to stare at her friends.

Great. Just great. First there was everything going on with her father. Now Jena and Dulcy's shock had turned to acute interest.

She sighed and pushed her curly hair back from her face. "Look, guys, I'm really not up for this right now."

Jena crossed her arms over her chest. "Funny, because we are."

"What's going on, Marie?" Dulcy asked.

Marie stepped to the table and scooped her things into her briefcase. "Can we talk about this tomorrow—"

The sound of raised voices coming from the lobby drew all of their attention.

First Jena, then Dulcy and Marie stepped toward the open conference room door. Given that she was a good four inches shorter than her friends, Marie had to do some maneuvering to see what was going on.

Just outside, by Mona's desk, Barry and Mona were arguing hotly. Marie tried to follow the rapid-fire words.

"I quit," Mona said, her voice ringing loud and clear.

Marie raised her brows. Well, that didn't take much to understand, did it?

All four of them watched as the woman who had been Barry Lomax's secretary for the past thirty years, and theirs for the past year, took her purse out of her desk drawer and strode toward the door. And that's where they all stayed well after Mona had left.

"Wow," Marie said.

Everyone nodded their agreement.

HERE THEY WERE TALKING about the U.S. Treasury Department and the questions the agents had asked Frank Bertelli Sr., and all Ian could think about was that he wanted to have some major sex with Marie so badly he hurt. And the fact that they were in public, sitting at a small round table in a very busy coffee shop located near their offices was not hindering his condition in the least.

It was hard to believe that only a day had passed since he'd last seen her...when he'd nudged her skirt up her remarkable thighs and peeked at her underwear. It seemed more like a week. And the truth of that made his mental state that much worse. He hadn't wanted anyone this bad since...well, since he'd had Marie eight years ago.

"My father's accountant's missing?" Marie asked after mulling over everything Ian had said.

Ian forced himself to concentrate on the matter at hand. Not an easy task when Marie had surprised him by showing up at the café in jeans and a T-shirt and a black leather blazer. She'd said she couldn't concentrate at the firm—something about a missing secretary and a general state of chaos—and had decided to work from home this afternoon. She looked hot. And he wanted to touch her.

He cleared his throat. "In a word, yes." He leaned forward and shook his leg in an effort to move his pulsing arousal to a more comfortable position. Thankfully his suit pants were baggy enough to conceal the sad shape he was in. "Your father says he didn't show up for work yesterday morning. Something I didn't find out until the questioning was well under way." He turned his coffee cup around to grasp the handle. "I had to do a bit of damage control when that little bit came out."

"Holy cow," Marie whispered.

Ian's gaze dropped to her mouth as she said the words. Damn, but she had a beautiful mouth. The kind of mouth that could take real good care of a guy if she put her mind to it.

"You can, um, say that again," he said, unsure if he was talking to himself or her.

Marie ran her fingers through her wild red hair several times, then sat back and blew a long breath out of those luscious lips. The fact that she was completely unaware of the carnal direction his thoughts had taken made her all the more attractive. Of course, not many people would be able to see beyond what he had just told her. Which was basically that her father was in deep doo-doo.

Her blue eyes focused on him. "Did they say what the reason was for the suspicion?"

Ian shrugged and took a long sip of his coffee. "Something about discrepancies on your father's business returns."

She grimaced.

"And, um, he was also questioned about his connection to someone out of Chicago."

"Who?"

"James Baldacci."

"Uncle Jimmy?"

Ian winced, her father's position looking dimmer and dimmer all the time. "You call Jimmy the Head 'uncle'?"

Marie looked genuinely perplexed as she leaned forward. "What do you mean, Jimmy the Head?"

She honestly didn't know.

Ian scratched his head then smoothed his hair back into place. "What do you know about James Baldacci?"

Marie's gaze narrowed. "Why did you just call him Jimmy the Head?"

"Answer my question first and then I'll answer yours."

She picked around the edges of her bran muffin, eating only the pieces that fell off onto her plate. "My father and Uncle Jimmy go back a ways. I think they came over from Italy together."

"Great."

"What does that mean?"

He debated telling her, then decided she'd probably get it out of him one way or another. "It means that Jimmy is called the Head because he heads up one of the most powerful crime families in the Midwest."

Marie had the olive-colored skin that went with her rich Mediterranean heritage. Not that you could tell at that moment because she'd gone as pale as copy paper. "You're kidding."

"I wish I was."

"Holy shit."

Holy cow to holy shit. Quite a jump for Marie even on a bad day. And fitting. Because Ian had thought exactly the same thing when the agents had asked Frankie Sr. about Jimmy, and Frankie had shrugged and explained that they were friends. Very good friends. Not something one usually went around bragging about, especially to U.S. Treasury agents.

"So what happened to my father's accountant?"

Ian finished off his coffee, then wiped his mouth with a napkin. "I think the treasury agents believe he's wearing cement boots at the bottom of a very large pond," he said from behind his napkin.

But Marie had heard him and looked about a flinch away from flinging her coffee into his face.

"You can't possibly believe that, can you?" she asked, color returning to her face in full.

"I didn't say that. I said I think the agents believe that."

She looked like she'd been physically struck. "Why that's stupid. Ridiculous. Ludicrous."

"It's fact."

She went silent and still, looking much like a statue as she stared at him in dawning realization.

Ian felt decidedly uncomfortable. All these years and never once had he thought that the joking rumors about Frank Bertelli were true. Don Bertelli, indeed. Hell, the morons among the kids his age had also habitually greeted the Schlachter kid down the street with a Nazi salute. Certainly none of them had ever truly believed he was a Nazi.

He absently rubbed his temples.

"Have they checked Uncle Nunzio's house?" Marie asked.

Ian knew that Frank's accountant was Nunzio Capeletti. "You call him uncle, too?"

Marie waved her hand. "Every male Italian friend of my parents is an uncle. Just like every female is aunt. It's just the way things work."

"I call none of my parents' friends uncle or aunt."

"You're not Italian." She pushed away her coffee cup and hardly eaten muffin. "And you're also not answering my question."

"Yeah, they checked your uncle Nunzio's house. Toothbrush was still wet. Yesterday's paper had been read and was still out on the kitchen table. Everything indicated he'd been there and had gone through his normal routine. Then, um, he just disappeared from the face of the Earth."

Marie stared at him, her mouth slightly agape. "And, of course, the first thing everyone thinks is that my father had him fit for cement boots. Because, after all, he is Italian, and everyone Italian is involved in the mob, right?''

Ian made a face. "Something like that."

"God, I can't believe this is happening. Again."

Ian scanned her face as she stared at a spot over his shoulder. "What do you mean, again?"

She shrugged then tucked her hair behind her ear. Ian's gaze was drawn to the long, sexy line of her neck. His mouth watered with the need to press his mouth there, at the base, then work his way up to the shell of her ear...

He shifted uncomfortably again, astounded that he was thinking the way he was given the nature of their conversation.

He should be the one fitted for cement boots.

His eyes widened. Maybe he would be if Don Bertelli ever found the little Irish boy from down the street had banged his daughter.

He cringed.

"What I mean is this," Marie said, waving her hand, clearly irritated. "My whole life I grew up with everyone talking to me with a sorry Brando imitation. 'Hey, Marie, your father gonna have me knocked off if he catches me talking to you?' 'Yo, Marie, find any ice picks missing lately?' Or my personal favorite, 'Hey, Marie, any dead bodies turn up in the freezer this morning?'"

Ian cracked a smile. "You do a pretty good Brando."

"That's because I heard it often enough." She sighed and slumped in her chair. "God, I thought all that...juvenile behavior was well behind me. I haven't even thought about Brando for the past five years." She absently shredded her napkin. "The only problem is that those idiot kids grew up to be treasury agents and are still spewing the same crap they used to when they were kids.''

Ian narrowed his eyes as he looked at her. He'd always been amazed by how strong she was despite her small size. Little Marie Bertelli could stand up to the biggest bully and cut him down to size with her sharp wit and her reasoning capabilities. It's probably what made her such a good attorney today.

And one hell of a desirable woman.

''I want to ask you something, Marie, before I have to get back to the office to meet a client,'' he said quietly, pushing his own coffee cup away. ''But I want you to promise you won't get angry with me.''

She blinked her beautiful baby blues, but didn't promise a thing.

''Is there even a remote possibility that…a slim chance that maybe…'' He trailed off, the words lodging in his throat at the growing look of suspicion on her face. ''Marie, is it possible that your father is a member of the mob?''

Ian braced himself for her response, distantly grateful that both their coffee cups were empty and hoping that a stale muffin couldn't do any major damage.

''What are you doing later?'' she asked.

Ian blinked. Not exactly the response he'd expected. ''How do you mean?''

''I mean that we,'' she leaned forward, pointed first to herself, then at him, ''you and me, we need to have a bit of a talk after we've a had a chance to think about everything we just said.''

He reached into his pocket, then tossed a tip to the table, his gaze glued to Marie's unreadable face. ''Will it involve sex?''

She looked a breath away from laughing. Which was definitely a good thing.

"No," she said clearly.

"Damn."

She slid her purse strap over her shoulder. "My place at six, okay?" she asked.

He nodded numbly and wrote down her address on the back of a clean napkin. "Six."

She got up. "Oh, and bring wine. Red."

Ian stared after her as she strode toward the door, feeling strangely like he'd just been sucker punched. Wine? He slowly folded up the napkin he'd written on, then slid the neat square into his inside jacket pocket. He was getting the distinct feeling that no didn't always mean no.

And even the hint of a possibility of sex with Marie shot his hormones through the roof.

He grabbed his empty coffee cup, then slowly counted backward from ten. He was afraid if he got up right away everyone in the place would know how much he was looking forward to having sex with one astoundingly sexy Marie Bertelli.

And how hopeful he was that he would rid himself of his burning need for Marie Bertelli for good.

5

IAN'S QUESTION HAD ECHOED through Marie's mind for the remainder of the afternoon. After repeated phone calls to her father's office at the first dry cleaner he'd opened thirty-five years ago had failed to turn him up, she'd called her mother, who had, as usual, created more questions than answers. Namely, questions about Frankie Jr. Her mother had asked if Frankie Jr. had seemed okay to her lately. Said he looked tired to her. And worried about something.

Given what Marie had on her mind, the last thing she wanted to worry about was her oldest brother.

She moved around in her kitchen, chopping fresh basil, peeling an onion and making a dinner she wasn't all that sure why she was making. Her mother had always told her that cooking always helped her think problems through more clearly. Somewhere down the line Marie had tried it and found that it worked.

And if there were ever a problem she needed to think through…

She brushed her hair from her forehead with the back of her hand, the question that had been haunting her all afternoon springing forth again.

Was her father in the mafia?

She nearly cut herself as she chopped an onion.

She'd asked her father that same question once. When she was eight and began to understand what all the teasing was about. She remembered the day clearly, because it bothered her to think that her father might be involved in an organization that had people knocked off for disagreeing with the way business was done.

Frank Bertelli Sr. had taken her by the hand as if he'd half-expected the question, lifted her up onto a tree limb while he leaned against the trunk. Then he'd patiently told her that the mafia was the creation of Hollywood producers, concocted for the movie-going public and that in no way was it a reality.

Even then, though, Marie could tell the difference between an answer and a nonanswer. So she'd asked the question again.

Frank Bertelli had been much younger then. Fit. And devastatingly attractive when he laughed. And he'd laughed then, calling her words of endearment in Italian, then telling her unequivocally, no. He wasn't in the mafia. He was a hardworking man trying to support his family the best way he knew how. Nothing more, nothing less.

But weren't those in the mafia just doing the same thing? she'd asked.

He'd tousled her hair and taken her down from the tree and told her yes, he supposed that was true. But none of them had a family that had been in the dry-cleaning business for three generations.

The answer had been enough for her then. And if she'd had any additional doubts over the years, she'd reasoned them away herself. After all, they didn't live in Chicago or New York or Vegas. What would the mob want with Albuquerque, New Mexico? Besides, no unexplained dead bodies popped up in the city's waterways. No stings ending in arrests of dozens of Italian-Americans was ever covered in the papers. Her family bonded with other Italian-Americans because they had a shared past, a cherished culture. Period.

She found herself tearing up and cursed the wretched onions as she added them to hot oil in a frying pan.

Uncle Jimmy was known as Jimmy the Head?

The doorbell rang. She glanced at the oven clock and frowned. Five thirty-five. Still a good deal before six and the time when Ian would arrive. She turned off the heat, wiped her hands on a towel, then headed for the door.

"You're early…"

Her words drifted off because it wasn't Ian standing in the hallway holding a bottle of wine. Rather, her brother Frankie Jr. leaned against the doorjamb and grinned at her.

"Hey, sis, what do you think about having a roommate for a few days?"

Marie stood frozen to the spot.

"Hey, what's that I smell?" he asked with a grin. "Are you cooking? Good. I'm starved."

He bumped into her shocked, rigid body as he passed into the apartment, his six foot three solid frame making her one-bedroom apartment seem much smaller than it had only moments before.

Frankie Jr.…at her house…staying for…how long did he say? A few days?

Blood slowly seeped back into Marie's limbs as she closed the door and began to lock it. Then, remembering the time and who else was due to arrive there in a few minutes, she pulled it open again and checked outside. The only movement was that of old Mr. Peabody peeking through a crack in his door at the activity outside Marie's door, his security chain in place.

Marie gave him a weak wave then closed the door

again and secured her own chain, only to unsecure it again.

She found Frankie Jr., six years her senior, in the kitchen, heating up the onion she had turned off. "You know it's not good for you to leave stuff like this. Ruins the flavor," he said.

She stared at him.

All three of the Bertelli boys looked exactly like their father. Thick dark hair. Shining brown eyes. And white flashing grins that put the "oo" in swoon. They would also be called boys until the day their father died. It was the way things were.

Unfortunately, it was Marie's experience that they all tended to act like boys as well. Hormone-ridden, clueless teenagers that wouldn't know the definition of the words respect and responsibility if she pointed it out to them in Webster's. Growing up she hadn't known a lick of privacy. And, of course, it had been impossible for her to date anyone casually, because the Bertelli boys didn't want their little sister sullied. If she was going to get married, they would choose the guy that would be their brother-in-law.

And Frankie Jr. was the worst of the three. He'd never really so much as talked to her than talked at her, presenting her with endless monologues on how a proper girl should act. If she found it ironic that the girls he'd dated acted nothing like the way he told her she should be, well, that was his business, he'd told her. Her job was to listen, not to question.

She'd kicked him in the shin the first time he'd told her that.

And, remarkably, she felt like kicking him in the shin now.

He was rifling through her refrigerator, then looked

over his shoulder at the dining room table. "What, no fresh tomatoes?"

"I was going to use canned," she said, closing the refrigerator, then shutting off the heat under the pan again.

"Hey, I was cooking here."

She pushed him to lean against the opposite cabinets, then crossed her arms. It didn't matter that he loomed over her by a good foot and that he probably weighed twice what she did. She and he were going to have words.

"What are you doing here, Frankie?" she asked evenly.

He looked at her as though she had just threatened him physically. "What? It's against the law for a brother to want to visit his sister?"

She squinted at him, imagining him without the innocent expression he wore as naturally as his skin.

"Did Mom send you here?"

The look of fear that crossed his face was priceless. It also did away with any fear she may have entertained that Frankie Jr. had been sent to keep an eye on her. She'd had some thoughts that perhaps the other night her parents had caught on to the attraction that arced between her and Ian, and her older brother had been sent to make sure nothing came of it.

He pointed a finger at her. "Mom doesn't know I'm here. And I'd appreciate it if you didn't tell her."

Marie twisted her lips, adding the two and two together in her head. Her mother's concern that something was worrying Frankie. And his standing in her kitchen right now.

Four years ago Frankie had married Antoinette Faretti, the daughter of a man who owned a chain of grocery stores in the greater Albuquerque area. In that four years they'd had two boys, Little Frankie III and Anthony. And while Marie had always wondered if the match had been arranged by the parents involved, her doubts had been mostly laid to rest when she'd caught Frankie Jr. and Toni going at it like dogs in heat almost every time she came across them alone.

So why, then, was her brother now standing in front of her afraid she might tell their mother about his presence?

Marie uncrossed her arms and sighed. "Okay, Frankie, what gives? You and Toni have a fight?"

He ran both hands through his cropped hair several times, then paced a short ways away. "I wouldn't call what went down a little while ago a fight. I'd more compare it to major combat."

"What did you do?"

He stared at her. "What? Why do I always have to be the one to blame?"

Marie shrugged. "Because you usually are. What happened?"

He tucked his chin against his muscular chest. "She thinks I'm banging my secretary."

Marie's eyes widened so far she was surprised her eyeballs didn't pop out. "Dottie?"

She envisioned the sixty-something secretary at the construction contracting company Frankie owned along with her other two brothers, none of them having opted to take the route their father had in the dry-cleaning business.

"No, not Dottie." He rolled his eyes as if addressing a particularly slow-witted child. "Dottie had a bout with pneumonia a month ago and up and retired on us."

Marie nodded. "Uh-huh."

He held his hands palms up and shrugged. "So we hired this girl...this woman..."

"Her name will do, Frankie."

"Lola. Lola Genesi."

Marie visibly flinched.

Frankie grinned. "And, oh man, is she ever hot. And when I say hot, I mean hot. When the temporary agency sent her over...well, every guy in the place went ape shit, you know? The first couple of days almost no work got done 'cause we were all too busy trying to figure out things to have her do so she'd have to bend over, you know?"

Idiot. "Go on," Marie reluctantly encouraged, hoping he was heading somewhere with this.

He sighed, all humor disappearing from his face. "Yeah, well, Toni didn't like her from the get-go."

"I wonder why."

Frankie stared at her. "What is it with you women?"

"Go on," she said again.

He stretched his neck. "Anyway, yesterday Toni found out what Lola used to do."

He stopped there. Marie hated to ask, but did anyway.

"And that is?"

"Strip."

Marie gaped at him.

He pointed a finger at her again. "Oh, no, don't you go giving me that look, too. I had enough of it from Toni." He dropped his arm. "The girl's got skills, Marie. I mean, real skills."

"I bet."

"What, do you women have a handbook or something? That's exactly what Toni said." He glared at her. "What's the matter with a woman who looks as hot as Lola having skills that don't include stripping? I mean, she took classes. Has a degree and everything. And she types twice as fast as Dottie ever did. And I can find stuff, you know, right where it's supposed to be. The customers like her. And before you say anything, even the women customers like her. And she raises morale around the place. No easy task in the middle of winter, I gotta tell you."

"And you told Toni this," she stated rather than asked.

"Of course I did."

"That's what I thought."

He stared at her blankly.

"Are you boinking her, Frankie?"

His mouth dropped open. "What kind of word is that for my little sister to use?"

She rolled her eyes to stare at the ceiling. "Answer my question."

He paused for a long moment, then all fight left his face. "No, Marie, I'm not. I mean, I guess I can understand why Toni might, you know, think like that. But I love my wife. The only person I'm interested in sleeping with is my wife. Why can't she understand that?"

"Maybe because you made Lola sound like the queen of the world while all she gets to hear is stuff like 'when's dinner going to be ready?' and 'did you wash my blue shirt?'"

It was obvious he wasn't following her.

She put her arm around his waist and started walking him toward the door. A glance told her it was five to six. Instead, she turned him back toward the kitchen table and sat him down. The last thing she needed right now was for Frankie to see Ian. Lord only knew what would happen.

"Sit down, Frank."

He did.

She patted him on the shoulder. "I've got to go out. Why don't you stay here, you know, for an hour or two?" She shook a finger at him. "No more. Then go back home to your wife and work this out. Tell her what you told me."

"What, about Lola?"

Dimwit. "No. About how you love her and that you wouldn't dream of sleeping with another woman."

He held up his hands. "I didn't say anything about not dreaming about them."

She whacked him on the arm. "I meant that as a figure of speech, dummy. Tell her you'd never sleep with another woman."

"Oh. Okay. That's the truth." He looked at her. "You think it will work?"

She smiled at him. The big lug. "Yeah, I think it will."

Just that moment, the doorbell rang.

Frank moved to get up, but Marie held him still. "Sit here. I'll get it."

She was relieved when he did as she asked.

IAN STARED DOWN AT THE bottle of wine in his hand, wondering if he'd brought the right kind. The guy at the wine shop had told him that for Italian food you could never go wrong with a good Chianti. But he didn't know that Marie was cooking Italian. Did Chianti go with meat loaf? Or fried chicken?

He raised his hand to knock at her apartment door when it swung open, and Marie, looking harried and nervous, stepped out into the hall, tightly grasping the door closed behind her.

"Go out to your car and wait for me."

Ian stared at her. "Well, hi, to you, too."

She waved off his attempt at humor. "Now. I'll explain when I come down."

"Okay," he said slowly.

She ducked back inside the door.

Ian stared at the closed wood and wondered what was going on. The door opened again.

"What kind of car do you drive?" she whispered.

"A silver Lexus SUV."

Her response was a roll of her eyes and the slamming of the door in his face again.

Ian scratched his head. Well, what in the hell was all that about?

Okay, so some time had passed since he'd actually been invited to have dinner at a woman's house, but he didn't think this qualified as normal date behavior. He didn't suppose this qualified as a date either, because Marie had said sex wouldn't be involved. And for a date to be a real date, sex had to at least be a possibility, no matter how remote. Otherwise it was two friends meeting to chew the fat.

He weighed the bottle in his hands, then let it slide so he held it by the neck as he turned toward the hall stairs. So he'd wait in the car. Good enough. He didn't know what she wanted to talk to him about anyway.

He wondered how much time he should give her. Five minutes? Ten? He stepped outside into the cool late-January night air. He didn't think it was a good idea for him to wait around any longer than that no matter how curious he was about her strange behavior.

He climbed into his Lexus and closed the door, then

sat for a long moment staring at the front of her apartment building. Seeing as the venue had changed, his prospects for any sex had just dropped exponentially. A restaurant was definitely not a place where one could get intimate. He glanced around the car. No. Not there, either. He didn't think he was that desperate yet.

He ignored that for the lie it was and thought about *his* place.

Definitely out. When he'd left a little while ago, his roommate Tyler Hammond was getting ready for a female visitor. A sign that he shouldn't go back there for at least the next few hours.

It made him curse his decision for having agreed to take on a roommate at all.

But when he'd returned from Chicago he'd had little choice. It was either live in a cheaper place until he could afford something better or take on a roommate.

He'd chosen the latter.

"You still have Illinois plates on your car."

Ian had been so wrapped up in his thoughts he hadn't even realized Marie had exited the apartment building and was now buckling her seat belt next to him.

"What?"

She was looking toward her apartment two floors up. "Oh, God," she said, slinking down in her seat. "Let's go."

Ian craned his neck to see who she was looking at. Marie slapped her hand across his chest. "Now."

He started the car, then put it into gear.

Five minutes into aimless driving, he finally looked at her. "Okay, I'm done waiting for an explanation you have yet to offer. What's going on?"

Marie turned from where she was looking through the back window. She took a deep breath, then collapsed against the seat. "A guest just up and landed on my doorstep."

"A guest?"

She looked at him. "Frankie Jr."

A horn blared. Ian jerked to find he'd drifted into the other lane.

"You're telling me," Marie said, although Ian hadn't made a comment one way or another. "A half hour ago he shows up saying he needs to stay for a couple of days because his wife thinks he's banging his secretary." She pushed her hair back and held it, the dim lights of the dash illuminating her sexy face. "God, I hope he didn't see you."

"Not any more than I'm hoping."

She grimaced at him. "Let's go to your place."

He skimmed her features while keeping a sharp eye on the road, trying to figure out if her motivation was sex. He decided it wasn't. "Not an option," he said.

She squinted at him, then seemed to realize something.

"No, it's not a woman. It's a roommate. A male roommate. A male roommate who happens to be entertaining a female even as we speak."

"You have a roommate?"

He shrugged. "I'm not exactly rolling in dough yet."

She gestured toward the car.

"My one indulgence."

"But the high-profile cases you've handled…"

"High on profile, low on cash." He glanced at her. "Think about it. None of my clients were members of the jet set."

She thought about it for a minute, then smiled. "Ah."

"Glad you're amused."

She shrugged deeper into her leather jacket. "Not amused, really. More surprised. I would have thought by now that you would be rolling in it."

He frowned. "So did I."

He felt her gaze on him in the dark, but didn't return it.

The truth was, he had planned to be financially well off by the time he was thirty. And by all rights he should have been. But when he'd accepted the position at the prestigious law firm in Chicago, he hadn't known that he'd be working eighty-hour weeks for little reward until he put his time in. And even then there was no guarantee that he'd ever be made junior much less senior partner at some point in the future.

He switched on the radio, the sound of a rock CD filling the interior of the car. Of course he chose not to think about the fact that he had a penchant for choosing cases that didn't exactly promise cold, hard cash. It was one of the reasons why the Chicago firm had ultimately let him go. Because he wasn't pulling in the revenue they'd figured he should have.

"Oh," he said, reaching beside him for the bottle he'd brought. "This is for you."

She took it and read the label. "I know just the place for this…"

MARIE KNEW SHE WAS TAKING a risk bringing Ian to Little Italia, a small Italian restaurant outside of town, but she figured if she behaved herself, when the news got back to her father, there would be no need for him to believe she was there for any other reason than an information-seeking mission. She glanced at her watch.

She figured her father had gotten word about a half hour ago, right after they'd walked in the door.

She and Ian sat in a corner booth in the back of the family-owned restaurant with its thick wood furniture, paneled walls and Chianti bottles with candles burning in them on the tables. The seats were upholstered in real leather, red, and the particular bench they were on curved so that she and Ian were actually sitting on the same seat but perpendicular to each other. Plates of antipasto were on the table as was a basket of fresh garlic bread.

Ian was watching a dark-haired waitress step to the cash register near the door where an older Italian man was on the phone.

"Is there an uncle around here somewhere, too?"

Marie half smiled. "That's Uncle Manny by the cash register. Aunt Rosita is probably supervising the kitchen." She twirled her wineglass holding the wine Ian had brought that she'd had the waiter open for them. "In fact, Uncle Manny's probably on the phone with my father now."

Ian's brows rose as he stared at her.

"Don't worry. I figure so long as we behave our-selves Dad will think this is a working dinner."

That brought a grin. "Who said I planned to behave myself?"

Marie's stomach bottomed out as he looked at her like they weren't seated in a busy restaurant but alone in a dimly lit bedroom. "I do," she said, clearing her throat when her voice came out as a husky whisper.

He responded to the sound rather than the words, his eyes darkening, his movements seeming slower some-how, more relaxed. And a relaxed Ian was a danger-ous one.

He sat back and stretched his arms along the back of the booth bench. ''It must have been fun being you growing up.'' He glanced around the place. ''There probably wasn't a place you could go, or a thing you could do that your family didn't know about.''

She took a sip of wine, the red liquid mellow against her tongue. ''Oh, I don't know. There was, um, a time or two when I escaped their attention.''

She looked at him and knew instantly that they were on the same page.

Her time in L.A. aside, her family had known nearly every detail of her life, except for the occasion when Ian had seduced her right out of her panties.

''What do you suppose they would have done had they known?'' he asked quietly.

She shrugged and pretended an interest in her wineglass. ''Oh, I don't know.'' She slanted him a gaze. ''Had you fitted for cement boots, maybe?''

His answering grin was fully loaded making her acutely aware of her damp thighs and the tingling low in her belly that had nothing to do with the wine and everything to do with thoughts of having another go at the man next to her.

She toyed with her antipasto.

''You don't eat very much, do you?''

''I wasn't aware you were paying attention.''

He shrugged nonchalantly. ''Just a casual observation.''

She put her fork down. ''I eat what I need to.''

''You're too skinny.''

''And you sound like my mother.''

He grinned. ''Smart woman, your mother. You should listen to her.''

That got a smile from her. Ian agreeing with her mother. Who would have thought?

Of course her amusement didn't change the fact that she tried to eat as little as she could without making herself ill. It was an obsession with her. A challenge of sorts to have a plate of great good in front of her and not have to eat it. She'd always been like that. It started at some point when she used to watch her brothers shovel their food down their throats. Depending which season it was and whether or not they were playing sports like football, she'd noted how drastically their weight fluctuated. Her mother always said that a man should have a little meat on his bones.

Marie had automatically taken that to mean that a woman shouldn't, despite her mother's generous shape.

Ian slowly chewed on a piece of garlic bread. She had smelled and touched the bread, and had even licked the garlic butter off her fingers, but she hadn't eaten it. "You know, you never answered my question earlier."

She shook her head. "I know."

He shifted so that he leaned his forearms against the table...strong, thick forearms peppered with dark hair and exposed to the elbow where he'd rolled up the sleeves of his shirt. "So?"

God, but the guy had a way about him. A sort of magnetism that drew her gaze, a charm that made her heart dip. She'd always known he was a serial dater. What bothered her was that *they* had never really dated. What had happened between them had, well, just happened. And afterward life had gone on as if nothing had happened.

She supposed that's what bothered her most about their encounters. She wasn't the type of girl to go around sleeping with men at the drop of a hat. Yet she'd slept with Ian without any promises.

She gave a mental shrug. She supposed it was good that there had been no lies either. She hadn't asked for more and he hadn't offered it.

She wondered what would have happened if either of them had asked for more. Would she be looking at him now pondering why she was so damn attracted to him? Or would she be cursing the day she ever showed him her underwear when she was eighteen and he'd taken her up on her offer?

"God, I'd love to know what you're thinking right now," Ian murmured, his expression dark and sexy.

She smiled at him. "Wouldn't you just."

She idly tucked her hair behind her ear, realizing she hadn't answered his question again—the one regarding her father's possible involvement in the mob. But right now she had other things on her mind. And until she chased them away she didn't think she'd be able to think straight.

Okay, so she wanted Ian so badly she nearly had to wipe drool off her chin just looking at him. What was wrong with taking what she wanted, the hell with the consequences? All this good-girl stuff was trying at times. The bad girl he had coaxed out before was yearning to make another appearance. And, darn it, she wanted to let her out. See what she had to say, what she wanted to do.

See if sex with Ian Kilborn was as good as she remembered it was.

"You know what I said about the no-sex thing earlier?" she said, making her mind up right then and there to forge ahead with what Bad Girl Marie wanted.

She virtually heard Ian swallow thickly. "Yeah."

"I changed my mind."

6

IAN CLAPPED HIS WIRELESS phone closed with a dark frown as Marie came back from the phone next to the cash register with an expression just as dark.

"Frankie Jr.'s still at my place."

"My roommate has moved his activities to his bedroom." He tucked his phone back into his pocket. "You don't want..."

She shook her head as she grasped the wine bottle. "Come on."

Ian wasn't about to ask where. All he knew was that Marie had changed her mind and the next round in the Marie and Ian match was as good as in the bag. He scooted out of the booth and followed her out the door, well aware that Uncle Manny was watching them closely.

Within minutes they were in the front seat of his car. "What did you—"

The rest of Ian's sentence died in his throat as Marie practically launched herself at him, tearing at the buttons on his shirt, tugging at the front of his pants, her mouth hot and wet and hungry.

He groaned low in his throat, a hunger rising to match hers. How long he had wanted this. He slid his hands to her slender hips, wishing he could rip the stick shift from between the seats so he could pull her onto his lap or lay her down across the seat. As it was, their attentions were administered over the armrest.

A light came on in the back of the already well-lit parking lot behind the restaurant. No doubt Marie's Uncle Manny playing amateur sleuth.

"Oh, God," Marie moaned.

Ian stared as the back door opened.

Marie scrambled back to her seat, her blouse bowing open. Had he done that? He didn't remember doing that. But obviously someone had. Ian caught his breath at the sight of her plain white bra and her small, pert breasts just beneath, her nipples pressing insistently against the thin fabric.

"Get out of here," Marie said for the second time that night.

Ian tried to shake himself out of his lust-induced lethargy. She opened her mouth but before she could speak, he said, "I know, I know. Now."

He turned the ignition, then shifted into reverse, skidding from the parking lot as Uncle Manny rushed out the door.

Marie pushed her hair back several times, appearing to have trouble catching her breath. She cursed. A rare occurrence that made Ian grin. "I feel like a goddamn teenager."

Unlike her, he kind of liked feeling like a kid again. Doing something forbidden. Hiding from the adults. Okay, so it was a little adolescent, but the rush of blood through his veins and his fully aroused, unsatisfied state, felt good. Damn good.

Especially since he planned to remedy his state as soon as humanly possible.

"A motel," he said.

She stared at him. "And I suppose you're going to

leave a little something on the table for me in the morning?''

''Right. Bad idea.''

''Real bad.''

''Pull over.''

Ian looked around the residential neighborhood. ''Where? What's here?''

''Nobody I know.''

His tires squealed as he broke to a stop. ''Good enough for me.''

He barely turned the engine off before Marie was all over him again.

Oh, yeah, he'd definitely missed this.

MARIE COULDN'T SEEM TO get enough of Ian. His mouth, his hands, his body. She couldn't stop kissing him, couldn't stop touching him, and couldn't seem to decide on a spot where she wanted him to touch her most.

She grasped his erection through his pants and gave a tiny gulp. She'd forgotten how big he was.

He pressed his palm against her right breast through her bra and she moaned.

''I...can't...seem...to...get...these...open...''

Ian restlessly moved her hand aside and popped open the clasp on his slacks then freed himself from his briefs. Marie licked her lips and took over from there.

Ian's hips bucked from his seat as she took him into her mouth. No licking, no stroking, she quickly took in as much of his length as she could and started sucking, loving the taste of him, the feel of him against her tongue.

''Holy shit,'' he gasped, pulling her head back with

an urgent tug of her hair. "You keep at that and I'm not going to have anything left for anything else."

She ran her fingers down the length of him with bold, thorough strokes. "What do you suggest?"

He tucked his fingers into the front of her jeans and tugged. "Get out of these. Now."

She readily obeyed, shifting and shimmying until the denim lay in a heap on the floor at her feet.

A strangled sound came from his direction. She glanced to find a predatory and completely provocative expression on his striking face.

"Damn, but you are so, so hot."

Marie glanced down at her completely unsexy plain white cotton underwear whose waistband stretched up past her navel.

"Get in the back," he ordered.

Marie moved to do just that, squeezing between the two seats and landing on the back bench seat at an awkward angle. She started to right herself but before she knew it Ian had stayed her with a hand to her stomach, holding her.

"Stay just like that," he said, not making a move to join her.

"But—"

"Shh."

She shimmied a bit in protest until he moved his other hand and ran it up the inside of her thigh, parting her to his gaze.

Saliva caught at the back of her throat. She didn't think she'd ever wanted to feel someone inside her so much.

He moved his fingers until they pressed against the cotton that lay against her crotch.

She gasped, heat pooling in her belly and surging toward that area he touched.

"So...sexy," he murmured.

Marie watched him through hooded eyes as he drew both hands up her parted thighs then pushed the fabric of her panties aside. He made a small sound as he gazed on her womanhood. He followed the rim of her damp crevice with his thumb then pressed the pad against her clitoris. Marie threw her head back and moaned, red-hot sensation pulsing through her bloodstream as he made small, tight circles around her hooded flesh. Then he pushed the hood back, baring her core to the cool night air. Seeming incapable of pulling air into her lungs, she cracked open her eyes just in time to watch him fasten his mouth around the very heart of her.

Marie tensed, reaching climax right then and there. She tried to move away from him but he held her tight against the seat with one hand, sucking and laving her with rapt attention. Then he thrust the fingers of his free hand deep inside her. Marie moaned, wondering at the ceaseless waves rippling over her, her muscles jerking and shuddering, rendered helpless against the onslaught.

Finally her womb stilled, leaving her completely boneless and liquid against the seat.

Ian removed his fingers, his grin one-hundred-percent satisfied male as he leaned back to look at her.

Marie couldn't help but smile back.

He turned toward the front seat.

She raised herself onto her elbows when she realized he was refastening his pants. "Where are you going?"

He glanced at her over his shoulder. "Taking you home, of course."

Of course? Of course?

Marie battled against the frustration blooming inside of her as he started the engine.

"But...but..."

"But what?" he asked, tilting the rearview mirror to look at where she still lay, spread-eagle, against the back seat.

Marie smacked her legs together and sat up straighter. "But I...we...you..."

"I can wait until next time."

Marie squinted at him as she moved her panties to cover her. What was this? A short time ago he couldn't wait to have sex with her. Well, okay, oral sex was sex but it wasn't intercourse. And now that he had a prime opportunity to have her, he was turning her down, telling her he could wait.

Was this a control issue? Was he playing some sort of sexual mind game in order to gain the upper hand in whatever was happening between them?

She was more than a little piqued as she squeezed through the seats to pluck her jeans from the floor then wriggled back into them while still in the back seat.

"What makes you think there's going to be a next time?" she asked, figuring that two could play at this particular game.

She didn't wait for an answer as she got out of the car, then got back into the passenger's seat where she put her shoes back on.

He pointed the car in the direction of her apartment.

Marie stifled a sound of pure frustration. He'd done it again. Proved to her, to himself, what power he had over her. And she'd just laid back and let him. Literally.

Again.

She fussed with her tangled hair. Okay, so she'd just had the most incredible orgasm she'd had in years, but that didn't make up for the fact that he'd set her up, tried to guarantee there would be a next time.

"There will be a next time," he said quietly.

She stared at him, intermittently illuminated by the passing headlights, feeling the incredible urge to whack him as she had Frankie Jr. earlier.

He grinned at her. "You know how I know?"

She didn't answer.

"Because you're too competitive to let things stand as they are."

"I am not competitive."

His answer was another grin.

This time she did make a strangled sound, her hands fisted in her lap until he pulled up in front of her apartment door.

She got out and slammed the car door, hearing his chuckle echo in her ears as she stomped away.

GOD, SHE WAS SEXY AS ALL get out when she was angry.

Ian sat silently in his car as he waited to make sure Marie got into her apartment building all right. Only after she had disappeared inside without looking back, and the door had closed behind her, did he allow himself to throw his head back against the headrest and groan.

Upsetting Marie had been the last thing on his mind when he'd decided to drive her home. But it had been either that or totally embarrassing himself. The truth was, seeing her draped over his back seat like that, her white, white panties contrasting against the dark interior, her thighs spread trustingly to him...well, he'd lost it. Just tasting her the way he had and hearing her soft cries had sent him careening right over the edge with her. He'd have some things to see to when he got home.

He dry-washed his face with his hands. Hell, he hadn't come like that from merely touching someone since...well, never. He'd always been the epitome of control, able to handle anything thrown his way.

And tonight, while going down on Marie, he had reached orgasm as easily as a thirteen-year-old boy looking at his first Playboy centerfold.

He cracked a grin. Boy, if Marie only knew the truth behind his urgency to drop her off. He rubbed his chin. Of course, he could have told her. She would likely have gotten a kick out of it. But she probably also would have viewed it as a challenge.

Why hadn't he let on? Why had he kept the information to himself and let her think he was toying with her?

And why had she immediately assumed he was toying with her?

Oh boy. Not exactly a topic to tackle when he needed to get home and climb into the shower.

Okay, so maybe he hadn't thought this thing all the way through. Normally, if he wanted something, he took it, never giving much thought to consequences or what happened afterward. He merely rode the wave.

But he already knew from the previous occasion with Marie that she wasn't a casual kind of girl, no matter how strongly she came on to him. She might play like she was a modern woman capable of casual sex, but when all was said and done she was as conservative as her family.

And him? How would tonight's events impact his working relationship with Marie's father?

Ian craned his neck and watched as her apartment light came on. He saw her silhouette as she pulled the curtain closed. Then he shifted into gear.

Normally, he wasn't so tuned in to what a woman was thinking. Understanding how *he* felt was where it began and ended for him. Not because he was uncompassionate. But because he was never drawn to understanding anyone. Until now. Until Marie.

He knew he'd hurt her before. Could see it in her eyes every time their paths crossed after they'd had sex. But what had happened between them before had been so mind-blowing, so overwhelming, he could do little more than run afterward. Pretend that she had been nothing more than a passing dalliance when she had been everything but.

Her family scared him, too.

He couldn't count the number of times when they were young that neighborhood boys had come away black and blue when they dared look at Marie the wrong way. He made a face. Maybe he was exaggerating. But not much. The Bertelli males were very protective of their baby sister. Hell, Frankie Jr. himself had told Ian that if any one of his friends ever tried anything funny with Marie that he'd personally make sure the guy lost his ability to father children.

Not a pretty picture.

Ian sank down in his chair. But there was also much more involved in his feelings for Marie. The sensation of losing time when he was with her. Or not so much losing it, but just not caring about it, so that when he discovered two hours had passed within a blink of an eye…well, that alone would be enough to scare the crap out of anyone, wouldn't it?

But then there were the other feelings. The ones that made him feel happy and sick all at once. He swore she was in his head when he was with her, forcing him to deal not only with his own confusing thoughts, but hers as well. And it was impossible that any man was equipped to handle that kind of pressure.

He ran his hand restlessly through his hair. Then, of course, there was the incredible guilt that pressed in around him and from inside him when he knew he had hurt her.

The same guilt he was feeling now.

He scowled. Hell, it was probably better that they hadn't had intercourse tonight. It was probably a good idea if he avoided ever having it with her again. Because all those feelings he hadn't been able to deal with in the past had surged back full force. And he wasn't any more equipped to handle them now than he had back then.

Damn, damn, damn.

He reached out and switched the CD back on, cranking up the volume until the singer drove all thought out of his head.

THE FOLLOWING MORNING Marie was in even worse shape than when Ian had dropped her off. She slammed the filing cabinet drawer, then rounded her desk and rifled through the drawers there. She couldn't find the blasted file on the Thompson case. She stalked out of her office and walked around and around Mona's desk trying to figure where else she could look. A loud sound from Barry's office startled her. She craned her neck to look inside the open doorway and found him mopping up liquid from his desktop, muttering curses under his breath.

She grabbed the box of tissues off Mona's desk and strode into his office. "You look like I feel," she said, plucking tissues from the box and laying them over the sopping mess.

Barry sighed and moved damaged files out of the way. He held up his coffee cup. "I've had this damn thing for over twenty years and it picked this morning to up and break on me."

Marie eyed the supersize cup and its broken handle in the shape of a deer antler. They silently worked together to clean up the mess on his desk while Marie stole glances at the man who was the senior partner of the firm.

She knew very little about Barry. Oh, she was aware that he and Dulcy went back to Dulcy's stretch at the New Mexico University's School of Law. That as a result of an embarrassing moment at Barry's expense, the two had formed a tight mentor-student relationship. But even Marie could see that Dulcy and Barry's connection was stronger than that. While Dulcy had a good relationship with her father, her friend seemed very fond of the man scooping soggy tissues into his wastebasket. From casual conversations over the years, and several more focused ones when the three women had signed on with Bartholomew Lomax, Marie knew that he'd been married three times and was a bit of a ladies' man. He'd even had a brief affair with Dulcy's...what would you call Beatrix Wheeler? Ex-mother-in-law-to-be? At any rate, the relationship hadn't lasted. And given the hours Barry had been putting in at the office lately, Marie suspected he wasn't seeing anyone at the moment.

Her thoughts drifted to their missing secretary Mona....

"Thanks," Barry said, drawing her gaze back to his face as she cleaned the last of the coffee from his desk. "The cleaning crew can see to the rest tonight, I guess."

"Sure," she said, wiping her hands. She looked at him a little closer, feeling sorry for him somehow. He looked forlorn. And appeared every one of his sixty-something years. "Is everything all right, Barry?"

He blinked his gray eyes at her.

Marie shrugged. "It's just that, well, you look like you could use someone to talk to this morning."

His grimace was endearing. "Maybe. But heaven knows what I would say." He shook his head. "My life is about as organized as my desk right about now."

Marie smiled softly. "Lives are supposed to be messy."

He chuckled. "Yeah, maybe."

Marie waited for him to say more, but he didn't. So she quietly cleared her throat. "Well, if you change your mind, you know where to find me."

He nodded. "Thanks."

"Don't mention it."

Marie ducked out of his office and had another go-round with Mona's desk, with little luck. She started heading back toward her office when the telephone rang. She eyed the extension, then looked around, half expecting Mona to emerge from the shadows to snatch it up.

She grimaced and picked up the receiver herself. "Hello," she said, wondering if she should have recited the firm name instead.

The caller was one of Dulcy's clients confirming a

meeting for the following day. Maria searched around on top of the desk until she found a message pad and jotted the info down as a deliveryman came into the reception area holding a potted cactus bearing a big red bow. She motioned for him to wait even as she took another call, this one needing a referral. Marie signed the delivery slip, waved at the deliveryman, then transferred the caller to Jena's office.

She smiled as she hung up the phone. Her friend would appreciate her for that one. The instant she took her hand from the receiver, the telephone started ringing again. She sought out then pressed the button that would send it and all forthcoming calls to the voicemail system. She was reasonably sure that there were directions for contacting each of the attorneys individually.

Finally free, she stared at the cactus she had accepted.

Her name was written across the front of the card in a large, loosely written letters. She reached out for it, then drew back, then reached for it again.

Ian had sent her a cactus.

She suppressed a laugh, not even bothering to read the card as she carried the plant to her office. His way of telling her she was prickly? She assumed so. She'd initially believed the delivery was for Mona. The thought caused her to ponder what could be going on between the womanizing senior partner and the bookish Mona. Which, of course, was absolutely the last thing she should have been thinking about right now. She glanced at her watch as she rounded her own desk and continued her search for the pesky missing case file. Her client was due for a meeting in a half an hour. If she didn't find the case file before then there would be nothing to meet about. She put the plant down on her desk and bent to look through her desk drawers again.

"God, you look like hell."

Marie nearly gave herself whiplash as she snapped upright to stare at where Jena stood in the doorway. "Gee, thanks."

Jena smiled. "Don't mention it."

Marie closed her desk drawer. "You wouldn't happen to know where the Thompson file is, would you?"

"Nope."

"Great."

She sighed and dropped into her chair. "Has anyone talked to Mona to find out when she's coming back? I swear, I haven't been able to find a thing since she quit yesterday. And somebody has to be out there to answer the phones and accept deliveries."

Jena sat down in one of the visitor chairs and crossed her long legs, looking chic and well turned out. Marie's frown deepened.

"I don't think she's coming back," Jena said.

Marie made an effort to improve her posture. "Sure, she is. What else would she do?"

Jena looked at her nails and shrugged. "Get another job. Specifically at a rival law office across town."

Marie's brows rose. "You're kidding me?"

"Uh-uh."

"Great," Marie grumbled again. "You know, you seem to know an awful lot about what's going on around here. What happened? You know, if you don't mind sharing?"

Jena dropped her hand to the chair arm and smiled. "Not until you tell me why you look like shit."

Marie pulled a legal pad in front of her, then slapped a pen down on top of it, her intention to try to wing the coming meeting and pray she found the file later. "Have I ever told you that you're good for the ego?"

Jena didn't rise to the bait. Then again, she rarely did. She was too busy waiting for everyone to rise to hers. Which they usually did. Marie being a prime candidate.

She gave a long-suffering sigh. "Frank Jr.'s staying at my place."

"What?" Jena uncrossed her legs, then leaned forward.

"What do you mean, 'what'? Last night I opened the door to find him standing on my doorstep. Toni thinks he's schtooping his secretary."

"Dottie?"

Marie shook her head. "Dottie retired last month. They've got a new secretary. Lola."

Jena laughed.

"Wait," Marie said as she held up a hand. "You haven't heard anything yet. It seems Lola is an ex-stripper who apparently took a couple of classes and can type like the wind."

"Is he?"

Marie frowned. "Is he what?"

"Schtooping her?"

"No. Of course not." She folded her hands across her stomach. "But Toni won't let him back into the house until he fires her."

"Sounds reasonable to me."

"Me too. But Frankie Jr. doesn't feel the same way."

Jena twisted her lips, her gaze taking in Marie's helter-skelter appearance, then the plant on the desk. "So that's why you look the way you do? Because one of your gorgeous brothers is staying with you?" She wrinkled her nose. "One of your gorgeous, caveman-like brothers?"

Marie felt the urge to hide the plant. "No. I look this way because when I got home last night, Frankie Jr. had taken over my bed and left me to sleep on the couch—which I found out the hard way isn't very comfortable, by the way—then commandeered the bathroom this morning, making me late for court."

"Where'd you go?"

"Go?"

"Uh-huh. Generally you have to go somewhere in order to come back." Jena leaned over to eyeball the card on the plant, then reached out for the card.

Marie snatched it from the plant, then put it in her desk drawer. "None of your business." She stared at the phone, willing it to ring. More specifically, willing the client she had a meeting with in…twenty minutes to call and reschedule their appointment. "I lived up to my end of the bargain. Now tell me what's up with Mona and Barry. I talked to him this morning and he looks…forlorn somehow."

"Forlorn?"

"For lack of a better word. Lack of sleep will do that to a person. Limit their vocabulary." She nodded. "Yeah, definitely forlorn."

"Good."

Marie was convinced her friend had taken a nosedive into the deep end of the pool. "I don't get you. How is Barry's being forlorn good?"

Jena looked through the window with the breathtaking view of the Sandia Mountains. "It's good because the old coot may be starting to come around. May even realize that he's in love with the woman who's been right there under his nose for the past three decades."

"Mona?"

"No, the cleaning woman. Of course, Mona." Jena smiled. "I know, shocking, isn't it? I can't believe I didn't catch on before now either. Well, before a couple of months ago. You know, I can't believe I didn't pick up on the undercurrents that have been sizzling between those two for the past ten months. Probably the last thirty years." She leaned forward and lowered her voice. "But a couple of months ago I make some off-the-cuff remark to Mona that she should update her appearance and she asks for advice." She made a face. "Well, okay, she hadn't so much asked for it than I offered it."

Marie shook her finger. "Now that's the shocking part," she teased.

They shared a smile. "Can I get on with my story or do you want to take any more cheap shots?"

Marie considered it. "I think I'm done. Continue."

"Anyway, before you know it I'm catching Barry and Mona going at it in the bathroom."

Marie's brows shot up. "The unisex?"

"The one and only. Up against the sink."

"TMI," Marie said, grimacing. "As in too much information for my innocent ears."

Jena made a sound of amusement.

"So they were…intimately involved, then."

"I don't know about how involved they were, but they were definitely intimate." The smile vanished from her face. "Unfortunately that's where my information ends." She shrugged. "Obviously something happened, things went sour and now…"

"We're without a damn good secretary," Marie finished.

"Yeah." Jena sighed. "I can't find anything either."

Marie tucked her hair behind her ear and decided she should call her client to reschedule. There was no point taking a meeting she couldn't perform well at. "Do you think I should call a temp agency and have them send someone over?"

"That would probably be a good idea."

Marie made a face and told herself to make sure to request the agency send over someone old enough to be her grandmother who didn't have a name like Lola.

She picked up the phone to call her client.

Jena waved her hand. "Hello. Aren't you forgetting something?"

"What?"

"The little matter of where you went last night? Or, more importantly, who you went there with?" She stared at the plant again.

Marie felt her face go hot, but she managed a smile. "Sorry, but I really, really need to make this call. Rain check?"

Jena stared at her.

"Mr. Gillette's office," Marie said to the receptionist who answered her call, waggling her fingers as Jena huffed from her office.

She sat back and smiled, really smiled, for the first time that morning.

As she waited for her call to be put through, she gazed at the plant again. A cactus. He'd sent her a cactus. She shook her head, then rifled around in her desk drawer for the card.

"Meet me at the Shady Pines Motel. Nine o'clock." He'd signed with a plain "I."

Marie read the words again, certain she was seeing things. He wasn't…there was no way…was he suggesting they meet at a motel?

Her back went up as she tossed the card back into her drawer and closed it, only to open it back up and stare at the offending card again.

Never. There was no way she was going to that seedy place for a quick roll in the hay. No matter how much her body screamed to finish what Ian had so skillfully started the night before.

She closed the drawer again, this time forcing herself to keep it closed.

No. Not a chance.

"Miss Bertelli?" the receptionist came back on the line. "Mr. Gillette has already left for his meeting with you. Shall I try to contact him on his wireless phone?"

Marie's grimace deepened. "No...that's all right. I'll talk to him when he arrives. Thank you."

She hung up the receiver, thinking that Gillette wasn't the only one she was going to have a talk with. Only there was no way she was going to speak to Ian at a hole-in-the-wall motel.

7

Aw, HELL. THIS PLACE WAS even worse than he'd thought it would be.

Ian stood in the middle of Room 7 at the Shady Pines Motel and wished he had thought to book the Ritz. He'd thought renting this room would be fun, fitting with the forbidden and secret nature of tonight. He glanced down at the bags of stuff he'd brought to try to improve the room, then at his watch. What he had and twenty minutes wasn't nearly enough time to make the place more appealing. In fact, he was afraid the only thing that could improve the room was a bull-dozer.

He put the bags down on the garish bedspread, hiding at least one of the countless cigarette burns marring the knobby surface, and stepped over the dirt-brown carpet he feared might have been beige at one time to the bathroom where the tub was helplessly stained, the thin yellowed towels the size of washcloths.

Oh, boy. He definitely wasn't going to win any points for this.

That was if Marie showed up at all.

He went back out and moved his bag to the dresser, then stripped off every last piece of linen on the sagging queen-size bed.

Okay, so he'd been desperate. He'd barely slept last night listening to his roommate do to his date what Ian wished he could do to Marie and could think of nothing but how he could go about doing that.

He paused, frowning at the jumbled thoughts. Did that even make any sense? No. But then again not much in his life did at the moment. And he didn't think it would until he figured out what was happening, and had been happening all these years, between him and Marie Bertelli. The only way he could do that was by spending time with her. And since spending time with her went hand in hand with wanting to bang her brains out…well, that had to be included as well.

He kicked the motel bedding into the closet, then remade the bed with the things he had brought.

Of course, the phone call from Frankie Sr. this morning hadn't improved his thinking capabilities any. Marie was right. Her "Uncle" Manny had contacted her father, passing on news of their "date" last night.

Ian had braced himself, waiting for a warning. Instead, Frankie had seemed more concerned that he not reveal to his daughter what was going down with the Treasury Department.

Ian frowned as he worked. He wasn't sure if he should be relieved or insulted that Frankie hadn't warned him against getting too close with his daughter. Either he was so preoccupied with what was happening he didn't give the matter another thought. Or, and Ian suspected this was the case, he didn't even give the possibility that he was dating material any credence.

Which meant what, exactly? It wasn't as if he was a different species. He was Irish. And a man to Marie's very enticing woman. Why wouldn't he be looked upon as dating material?

He caught the ridiculous direction of his thoughts and looked at his watch. Five minutes.

Would she come? He realized he was still wearing his business suit, due to a long dinner with a client and the shopping he'd had to do. He shrugged out of the jacket, pulled off his tie then rolled up the sleeves. It wouldn't do for him to look too confident.

He glanced around the transformed room.

Too late…

ROOM 7.

Marie sat in her Mustang in the parking lot of the Shady Pines Motel, alternately squeezing then releasing the steering wheel and wondering just what in the hell she was doing there.

Voices drew her attention. She watched as a couple exited Room 8. A tall, skinny man in his fifties wearing a business suit and a young, provocatively dressed Latina walked together but apart. It was obvious that what had just passed between the two of them in that room had been all business and very little pleasure.

The girl kissed the guy and grabbed his genitals. Marie cringed. Okay, maybe the guy had had fun.

Just sitting outside the place made Marie feel…dirty somehow. Sure, she had passed the place often enough. Hadn't even had to look up the address to know how to get there. Everyone in Albuquerque probably knew where the place was. But it was one thing to pass it and quite another to actually rent a room there.

She swallowed hard, admitting that something other than disgust also slunk through her bloodstream. A deep, dark simmering sense of the forbidden. Of doing something she usually wouldn't be caught dead doing. Of taking a step onto the wild side.

A shiver ran over her skin, tightening her nipples and making her clench her thighs together.

Okay, so maybe the prospect of meeting Ian in this seedy joint did excite her a little. Okay, more than a little. The surprising reaction was what had brought her this far, to sit in her Mustang staring at Room 7 and his Lexus parked outside.

Behind her car, the tawdry green neon sign blinked on and off advertising there were no vacancies, only the "n" part was burned out so what remained was "o" vacancies.

Marie gave a nervous laugh and slid her keys from her ignition.

She was going to do this. She knew it the moment she'd received that card, no matter her initial reaction. She and Ian had some unfinished business, although not the kind conducted by the pair she'd just seen. No, what existed between her and Ian was far more complicated. And far more confusing.

Marie got out of the car, only then wishing she had worn something other than her business suit. But to convince Frankie Jr.—who was still frustratingly ensconced in her apartment and was even this moment flicking her remote between a hockey and a basketball game while he ate everything in her cupboards and knocked back a few of the beers he'd bought—that she was going to a business meeting, she'd had to dress the part.

Interestingly enough, he hadn't even given her a second glance. Which really surprised her. Where was the grilling on where she was going, who she was going to be with and when she would be back? She slung her purse over her shoulder then held it tightly against her side lest any purse-snatchers be lurking nearby. She'd like to put Frankie Jr.'s uncharacteristic behavior down to his finally growing mature enough to recognize that she was a grown woman capable of making her own decisions. But one had only to look at him, and the mess he was making out of his life, to know that there was no way that was the reason for his waving her out of the apartment with little more than "have a good time."

Marie drew parallel with the motel room door and started to slow, only to pass by it. She curled her hands into fists as she stepped over the cracked pavement and tried to ignore the threadbare curtains covering each of the windows she passed. At the end of the walk was a soda machine. She rummaged in her purse for loose change, noted the inflated price, then rummaged around for more change before discovering the only selection available was tonic water. She scowled. Why was it that the only thing ever left in these darn machines was that? And why was the unpopular drink even a selection to begin with? Didn't it make more sense to put a second row of the more popular beverages?

She started when the dropping can made a loud clang in the otherwise quiet night. Maybe the company didn't know it was so unpopular because, hey, they sold, didn't they? They just didn't know the reason it sold was that there was nothing left to choose from.

She turned back toward Room 7 and took a deep breath. Yep, yep, yep. She'd pretty much exhausted her well of excuses not to go into the room, short of getting back into her car and leaving. She straightened her skirt and headed for the door. She realized she was going to pass it again when it opened. She started, then turned to see Ian leaning against the jamb grinning at her. "Going to complain to the manager about the soda selection?" he asked.

Marie suddenly had trouble swallowing. Ian looked

better than any man had a right to, considering their surroundings. He looked handsome and clean and so very inviting.

"Um, hi," she said inanely.

His grin widened. "Hi, yourself." He moved aside. "Why don't you come in?"

Marie hesitated, preparing herself for the smell of mildew and other myriad scents she'd prefer not to identify. "I can't believe you invited me to a place so..." she stepped over the threshold and smelled...was that strawberries? Yes, very definitely strawberries mingled with...Lysol. "Seedy," she finished with a whisper.

She blinked to adjust her eyesight to the dimness of the room, then widened them. Candlelight flickered everywhere from candles of every size, shape and color. A black sheet had been thrown over the ratty curtains, and the bed...

Wow.

Nowhere to be seen were the normal motel fare. Instead she stared at a thick black silk comforter folded back to reveal red silk sheets with several thick, fluffy pillows hiding most of the headboard.

Her heart pounded thickly in her chest as she stepped forward, letting her purse slide from her shoulder and onto the floor.

"Wow," she murmured the word aloud.

Ian had closed the door and stood directly behind her. "Would you like a drink?"

Marie absently held up the can of tonic water. "I brought my own."

His low chuckle made her shudder while the feel of his hands skimming down her arms sent shivers skittering everywhere. He plucked the can from her hand. "Maybe you can finish it later."

She nodded dumbly as he stepped to a long set of drawers that he'd draped with another dark sheet and poured her a glass of white wine from a bottle cooling in the room's ice bucket. Marie heard the music, but couldn't locate the source of it. She did, however, recognize the low, sensual sounds of David Sanborn's sax.

She accepted the glass of wine, oddly touched that Ian had gone to so much trouble to make the room more acceptable. Acceptable? It was fantastic.

She could barely force a sip of wine down her tight throat before she put the glass down on the end table...then launched herself at Ian.

YES, IAN THOUGHT, "WOW" just about covered it.

He stumbled backward as Marie slammed against him, then planted his feet solidly on the floor, all too eager to forget small talk and get straight to the reason both of them were there in the first place.

Clothes went flying everywhere, some of them probably ruined forever if the tearing sounds he heard were any indication. But he couldn't bring himself to care. All he could do was focus on the thick pulsing of his heart, the sweet scent of Marie's hair against his nose and the silken feel of her skin under his hands.

His countless fantasies of this moment didn't come anywhere near the real thing. And, oh boy, had he had the time over the years to hone and embellish his fantasies.

Finally, they were both completely nude and Marie sighed against him, as if she'd been looking forward to this moment just as much as he had.

Ian knew a moment of pause as he skimmed his

hands over her bare back and the sweet curve of her bottom. He hauled his mouth from hers and looked down at her—at the way her skin was already flushed with heat, her small breasts heaving as she tried to catch her breath. His own breath caught in his throat.

He'd never seen her completely naked before. Never gazed at her in all her bare glory. Like last night, he'd seen bits and pieces and flashes, but never the whole package all at once. And now that he could...well, he was going to take his time to appreciate the view.

Marie moved to cover herself with her hands. He caught her wrists. ''Please don't. I just want to...look at you.''

He heard her thick swallow, but she didn't fight him as he released his grasp on her and her arms dropped back down to her sides.

Good Lord, but she was perfect. From the curve of her neck, the slope of her breasts and the soft curls between her thighs, to her nicely shaped feet, she was perfect.

He lifted his fingers to her right breast, mildly surprised to find his hand shaking as he lightly touched the dark tip, fascinated as the skin contracted and puckered and protruded, responding to his touch and seeming to beg for more attention.

He made a sound deep in his throat as he weighed the flesh in his palm, then lifted his other hand to do the same to her other breast, brushing his thumbs over the stiff nubs. She gasped, all stiffness leaving her body as he bent his head and sucked one of her nipples deep into his mouth, laving it with his tongue, then leisurely followed with the other. No jealous breasts allowed.

Marie's knees buckled and Ian caught her up in his arm, the rasp of her bare skin against his sending a quake through him. He tunneled his hands up under her thick hair and tilted her head back, staring down into her flushed face, knowing that he was the one who had made her look like that. From her swollen lips to her half-lidded eyes, he had evoked her highly aroused state, and with very little effort. And the knowledge aroused him all the more.

"You're a tease," Marie whispered, raking her fingers up and down his back.

"You're fun to tease," he answered, grabbing her bottom and pulling her flush against his rock-hard erection.

She gasped at the state of his arousal and he chuckled.

"Surely you're not surprised."

She gave him a half smile. "Pleasantly."

He grabbed hold of her slender hips and tossed her to the mattress beside them, causing her to cry out. Before she could bounce a second time, he covered her skin with his, reveling in the feel of her against him, and the simple fact that they were alone.

Finally.

It was enough to make him close his eyes and revel for a moment.

But Marie was having none of that. She curved her feet around his calves so that his hardness was cradled in her soft wetness. It was all he could do to pull back enough to sheathe himself with one of the condoms he'd put on the side table, and then he repositioned himself. A low, sultry moan escaped her lips and Ian nearly lost it right then and there.

What this one woman did to him boggled the mind. He felt like all control had left his hands the moment she stepped into the room. He was no longer responsible for his actions and had absolutely no say so in his body's response.

He smoothed her hair back from her face again and again, staring intently into her eyes to pull himself back from the brink. But seeing her huge pupils nearly taking over the blue of her irises, and watching her take shallow panting breaths, wasn't helping any.

"If you keep looking at me like that, it's going to be over before we've begun."

She smiled at him in a way that made his gut clench in preparation for climax.

Ian gave a low growl and lifted himself up so he could turn her over. She made a sound of surprise, but he didn't give her time to catch her breath as he pulled her hips back against him. He parted her farther, opening her sweet folds of swollen flesh, then fit the knob of his arousal against her slick opening. If he thought it would be easier this way, he was sorely mistaken. Her incredible desire for him was just as evident in this position, in her swollen genitalia, her unconscious rocking and the soft sounds she made deep in her throat.

"Please," she rasped, clenching the red silk sheets in her fists. "Please, Ian. I...can't bear it."

The only thing more stimulating than wanting a woman as much as he wanted her was knowing that she wanted him just as much. He slowly pressed inside her tight flesh. She arched her back and strained back against him, hungry for more. It took every ounce of the little control he had to keep from surging all the way home. Instead, he pulled out again, watching her engorged flesh contract in protest.

Marie buried her face in the sheets and gave a muffled scream of frustration. Ian released his grip on one of her hips and ran his palm the length of her well-defined spine. The instant her head came back up, he filled her again. This time to the hilt.

Her low moan swirled around and around him, matching the tremors racking his body, heightening them, until he teetered on the very brink he was trying to evade. Marie regained her bearings before he did and she bucked against him. He held her hips tight.

"Stay still a minute."

She did as he asked, but he wasn't sure if it was a conscious decision or if she needed the time to catch her own breath. He ran his hands over the delectable curve of her bottom again and again, commanding himself to pull back. He snaked one of his hands around her waist and up her flat stomach to pluck at her breasts. Her dripping muscles contracted around him and he thrust once, then twice, then again. He moved his hands to tightly grasp her hips from behind, positioning his thumbs near her shallow crevice and parting her so he could watch himself disappear inside her, then exit again, glistening with her desire.

It seemed he had fantasized about having sex with Marie in just this way, but he hadn't factored in the human element. Namely, his own thundering need to give himself over to the orgasm threatening to erupt. On the previous occasion, they hadn't had the luxury of time or accommodating surroundings, so their quick finish, he thought, had been necessary. Only he was finding that where they were, or how long they had, had absolutely no impact on where they were heading. It was all he could do not to ram into her like nobody's business until climax forced him to stop. He clenched his teeth as he stroked her deeply. But, damn it, he was going to take his time now.

He pulled her up with him so that he was now sitting with her on his lap, but with her back to his front, his hands framing and squeezing her breasts as she shuddered around him.

"Open your eyes, Marie."

She slowly did as he bid and met his gaze in the mirror on the opposite wall that threw their erotic coupling back at them. Their position showed everything. Her damp, fleecy curls and swollen flesh and his rock-hard erection disappearing inside of her.

He tweaked her nipples and she gasped, her mouth a soft mew of surprise. Then she reached back, bracing her hands on his arms, and lifted herself up, her gaze riveted to the image in the mirror as she slid back down again.

Ian groaned as he grasped her hips and brought her down again, hard, causing her breasts to sway. She cried out and he brought her down again and again, finding a hard driving rhythm that chased a moan from her throat with every thrust. Need gathered in his groin like a tornado out of control as he slid his fingers toward the V of her legs, finding the petal-soft folds there and parting them until her hooded flesh was visible in the mirror. He watched her watching him even as they kept up the brutal pace. Then he pressed his thumb against her molten core, causing her muscles to violently contract around him and she stiffened in orgasm.

Ian tightly clenched his teeth, reveling in the feeling of her coming, the evidence of passion all around him, grabbing him, claiming him, possessing him. Before she had stopped, he plucked her off his lap and laid her on her back, parting her thighs for him and driving all the way home, flesh slapping against flesh, cries melding with cries, until she came again and he chased right after her.

Long moments later, Ian's throat burned with his urgent efforts to pull in air, and his legs trembled with the effort to hold himself aloft from her. Marie twined her legs with his, aftershocks rocking her body as she kissed and bit at his shoulder, her cheeks damp with…were those tears?

Ian rolled over onto his side, pulling her with him.

"Oh, God, Marie," he murmured, smoothing her hair back. "Did I hurt you?"

She searched his face and gave a soft laugh. "Hurt me?" she repeated. She leaned forward and kissed him deeply, then kissed him again as if she'd never be able to kiss him enough, the salt of her tears mingling with the heat of her mouth. "Oh, no, Ian. You didn't hurt me. You've just given me one of the most incredible orgasms I've ever had in my life."

It took a moment for the words to sink. For Ian to put what she said together with the complete look of rapture on her face. He lay there for a long time drinking in her exquisite expression, memorizing every line and angle and crevice. Incredible. While he enjoyed knowing he was responsible for her pleasure, a warning bell went off in the back of his mind. An alarm telling him to watch out, be careful, that the slope he was on was slippery indeed.

Ian forcefully ignored it and grinned. "Marie, baby, you ain't seen nothing yet."

MARIE SLOWLY WOKE UP THE following morning, every muscle drained, a smile plastered on her face. Sex. Amazing sex. Made even more amazing because she'd had it with Ian, the man who had occupied so much of her thoughts for so long and had proved to her that reality was even better than fantasy. More than that, she couldn't help thinking that his consideration for her, his infinite patience and attention to every last erotic detail, also proved that what he felt went well beyond the bed.

Then she realized she was still in that bed, in the motel room and that Ian was still next to her.

Holy shit, she thought, extricating herself from where her arms and legs were tangled with his and leaping from bed. Her heart pounded in her chest but this time it had nothing to do with mind-blowing sex. Rather she was trying to find the clock or her watch, anything that would tell her what time it was.

She finally found the bedside digital clock under one of the pillows. Seven.

"Holy shit!" she said aloud this time, rushing first one way, then the other, knowing she should be doing something but completely at a loss as to what.

Movement on the bed. She stopped long enough to watch Ian prop an arm behind his head and grin at her. "Going somewhere?"

Marie stared at him, speechless, then stalked to the curtains where she pulled off the sheet, then opened the disgusting green curtains underneath. "Uh, yeah."

"Holy shit," Ian mimicked her when he saw daylight, leaping from the other side of the bed and rushing around with her.

Neither of them said anything for long minutes as they hurriedly gathered their clothes, nearly bumping into each other, then going around as they put themselves back together.

Although Marie felt strangely like there were a few important pieces missing. Or maybe not missing.

Changed. They had changed. She stood in front of the mirror and tried to put her hair in some sort of order, then wet her finger and rubbed at a spot of mascara under her left eye.

Despite the morning panic, she felt…exhilarated somehow. Reborn. And merely looking at Ian as he jumped into his pants and did them up, the well-defined ripple of his abdomen moving as he pulled up the zipper, filled her with need all over again.

He met her gaze in the mirror. ''Frankie Jr. go home yet?''

She blinked at him. ''Um, no. Toni won't let him back in the house until he fires his secretary. Something he refuses to do.''

Ian stared at her dumbly.

Marie waved her hand and reached for her coat. ''Long story. I'll explain it to you later. That is if my family doesn't kill me before then.''

She rushed for the door. Ian caught her arm and hauled her to his bare chest. She gasped when their bodies made contact. Then he kissed her. Deeply.

Despite the adrenaline crashing through her system, Marie's knees went weak.

Ian pulled his head back. ''Same time, same place, tonight?''

Marie looked around the room. ''I don't know…''

He slid his hand between them and grabbed her throbbing womanhood. She could feel herself grow instantly damp.

''Okay,'' she said quickly.

He grinned. ''That's more like it.''

She wriggled from his grasp, gave him one last kiss,

then hurried from the room, closing the door after herself. The cool late-January breeze was crisp against her skin. She took a deep breath and wondered exactly what she was getting herself into.

8

THE MORE SEX IAN HAD WITH Marie, the more he wanted. They'd met at the motel no fewer than five more times in Room 7 and yet all Ian could think of was getting back there.

He stuck the Frankie Bertelli Sr. case file into his briefcase and snapped it closed, wondering if it was possible he might never get sick of sex with her. He thought about his father and mother, who were still married after nearly forty years and living happily in an exclusive community an hour outside town. Marie's own parents had also been married a good long time.

He absently scratched his head. Did his father still want his mother sexually? He tossed that question out as soon as it sprung into his mind. Personally, he didn't want to think about his parents' sex lives, even though they'd had ten kids all told and therefore obviously had had a very active one.

Then there was Frankie Sr. and Francesca. Bearable to think about but only marginally. Funny, but his guess would be that Frank and Francesca still had a very healthy sex life. He'd witnessed Frank playfully swat his wife's bottom. Saw the covert winks Francesca gave her husband during dinner that made him uncomfortable because they seemed so…suggestive somehow.

He got up from his chair and felt his spine snap

straight. Of course, he was in no way thinking of him and Marie and marriage in the same sentence. To even link them all together was…preposterous. Farfetched. Impossible.

The question "why?" popped into his head and he threw it out as quickly as the question on his parents' sex life.

Because. Period.

He pressed his intercom button. "Cathy, I'm heading out to my meeting with Mr. Bertelli at the Treasury Department. Hold my calls, will you?"

After the receptionist told him she would, he released the button, then headed for the door.

Today was the agreed upon date that Frankie Sr. was to hand over his accounting books to the U.S. Treasury Department. The prospect both excited and disturbed him. This could possibly end up being one of his most important cases to date, not only from a personal standpoint, but a professional one. His bid for a full partnership with the firm was within his reach. Was he jeopardizing it with his relationship with Marie? Not only was she Frankie's daughter, but he was so damn distracted he found it hard to remember whether he'd locked his car doors, much less if he was covering all the bases in the case.

But in order to cover those bases, he first needed to know what they all were. And toward that end, he was going over to the main dry cleaner where Frankie had his office, make sure they had everything they needed, then they would drive downtown together.

And Marie was going to "accidentally" stop by the dry cleaner with an armful of clothes.

Ian flinched.

Okay, so he was weak when it came to keeping anything from Marie that she wanted to know. In fact, over the past few nights of meeting her in Room 7, their own personal love shack, he had not only come to understand that important fact but was learning how to milk it for his own benefit. And, oh boy, had he ever used it last night and received the most remarkable blowjob of his life. Just thinking about Marie's mouth on him made him hard all over again. Not good, considering a good seven hours separated the present from the time he would meet her back at the motel.

He rode the elevator down to the garage, absently rubbing the back of his neck as it descended. He'd been feeling apprehensive all morning. At first he'd thought it was because Marie would be showing up at the dry cleaner and he wasn't all that sure how Frankie would feel about that. But he'd finally accepted that wasn't the cause. Rather, he was afraid the information the firm's contracted private dick had faxed Ian first thing this morning was to blame for his uneasiness.

No new information on accountant Nunzio's whereabouts. But his car had turned up. In the junkyard, of all places. Worse, traces of blood had been found in the front seat and on the steering wheel. The private detective had sent a sample to a private lab for DNA mapping and comparison against hair follicle samples taken from Nunzio's brush—action Ian was certain the treasury agents had either already taken or would take now. On a positive note, the dick had told him there was no reason to believe that the agents had located the car yet because the junkyard manager hadn't known any of the details himself aside from that it had been towed there the day Nunzio had come up missing.

Ian swallowed hard. If Nunzio was wearing cement boots at the bottom of a pond, why would his car be totaled and evidence of blood be left behind? Had he known what was coming and tried to outrun his assailants?

The whole situation made Ian almost sick to his stomach. While he was relatively sure that Frankie Sr. was no mobster, there remained that tiny part of him that wondered if he was.

And wondered what would happen to him when Frankie Sr. found out he was boinking his daughter in a seedy motel across town every night.

He massaged the bridge of his nose, every image from every mob movie he'd ever seen careening through his mind. Meat hooks—wasn't one of Marie's "uncles" a butcher? Baseball bats—hadn't all of the Bertelli boys played baseball? People being buried in the desert outside Vegas—he refused to look beyond the Sandia Mountains to where plenty of desert existed, and instead told himself to knock it off.

Ten minutes later, Ian pulled into the parking lot beside the original dry cleaners Frankie Bertelli had opened thirty-five years ago, before there was even a junior to speak of. And before there existed the ten other sites located around the city and in Santa Fe. He climbed from his car and closed the door, scanning the exterior of the old brick building. It probably looked pretty much the same way it had back in the old days. No modern updates. No fancy neon sign. No advertisements for one-hour service. A plain white and black plaque hung above the glass door that read "Bertelli's Dry Cleaners." That was it.

He hadn't noticed Marie's Mustang parked in the lot so he supposed he should feel relieved she hadn't shown up yet.

Still, being in a suspected mobster's place of business on what looked like a slow day to get together his financial records...

Ian got the sick feeling all over again.

He pulled open the door and stepped inside to find no one in sight on the other side of the counter. There was no cowbell or anything to announce his arrival. Instead, a concierge's bell sat on the counter.

This was how it always started in the movies. Bright, young attorney unwittingly represents a mob figure and gets pulled into the mob himself, endangering the lives of everyone around him. And that wasn't saying anything about his own life.

Ian planted his feet on the floor and held his briefcase with both hands similar to the way a movie character might. Okay, so the prospect of being around the mob, much less being a part of it, intrigued him a little. Okay, a lot. Hey, when you were part of the family, you were part of the family. Nobody messed with you. And you were respected.

He grimaced. Of course, no one messed with him now. And as far as he knew he was already pretty well respected.

Still, just the thought of the illicit lifestyle kicked up his adrenaline flow and made him feel a bit taller.

"Ian!"

He nearly leapt straight out of his shoes at the sound of Frankie Sr.'s voice emerging from the back. So much for being mob material.

"How long you been waiting? You should have rung the bell."

Ian was never quite sure what to do whenever Frankie Sr. hugged him. He managed an awkward return pat on the back, thinking he was safe so long as Frank didn't give him the infamous kiss of death. If he ever got one of those...well, he'd probably die of a cardiac arrest right then and there.

"That's okay," Ian said, grinning at him. "I just got here."

Frankie Bertelli Sr. was a bear of a man with the charm of three men. He instantly made you comfortable with his amiable behavior and uncomplicated expressions. What you saw was what you got.

But did some of what Ian saw include the mob?

Frankie Sr. headed toward the back again. "Come on. The office's this way."

Ian looked behind him. "Doesn't someone usually watch the front? You know, man the counter?"

Frankie waved at him. "I used to have a girl out there, but this place, well, she don't do so much business anymore, you know? I take care of whatever comes through the door."

Ian nodded and followed him past the counter, then the concealing wall into the working area of the cleaners. Only nobody was working. While a number of plastic-bagged clothes, presumably already cleaned and waiting to be picked up, hung from hooks to his right, to his left was another scene straight from a movie. A round table was set up and around it sat five men of Italian heritage in the middle of a card game, a cloud of cigarette and cigar smoke billowing around them.

"Guys, I want you to meet my attorney. Ian, this here's the guys."

The guys.

Ian smiled and shook hands with each of them.

He only hoped that in "guys" Frankie didn't mean wiseguys....

IT WASN'T OFTEN THAT Marie lied to her father, so she wasn't so sure about her chances of pulling this one off. But if she was going to force his hand, get him to tell her what was really going on, this was a prime opportunity she couldn't pass up.

She stepped inside the receiving area of the dry cleaner and draped her clothes over the counter. Truth was that while she was secretly sure her father was proud of her and her accomplishments, she was tired of him leaving her in the dark. If something was happening to him, it was a family matter, and she was a member of the family. It was as simple as that. And she wanted to help.

She couldn't do that if he refused to let her.

"Papa?" She stepped past the counter and back into the working area. Growing up, she had spent a lot of time here. One summer she had actually worked there. But mostly she had hung out in order to spend some time with her father.

This branch hadn't always been this quiet. Before everyone gravitated to the more modern facilities the other chains offered, this main store had kept up a booming business. At least up until three years ago when they saw a steep decline in foot traffic. But here was where her father had first opened the doors and here was where he would always have his office, he'd once told her.

"Marie! Hey, look, guys. It's Marie."

She slowed her step as she came to stand in front of the card table that was as much a fixture around the place as the front counter. And the five men who surrounded it were as much a part of her family as her brothers. "Hi, Uncle Vinnie," she said and kissed him on the cheek, then greeted her uncles, Gino, John, Chris and Fabio, the same way.

"Marie!" her father called out.

She glanced up to find him standing in his office door next to Ian who was eyeing her in a way she wasn't sure she was comfortable with.

Her father elbowed Ian. "Look, it's my daughter Marie."

She went to him and gave him a kiss and hug, gazing at Ian over her father's wide shoulders.

"Uncles?" he mouthed.

She smiled at him.

"You said hi to everybody?" her father asked.

"Of course I did."

"Good. Good." He tucked his chin into his chest and looked at her in that way he used to when she was a kid and had done something she should have known better than to do. "Now tell me what you're doing down here."

Her uncle Vinnie made a sound of disapproval. "What? A daughter can't visit her father, Frankie?"

"You ask that question 'cause you don't know my daughter very well." He shook his head. "Too big of a coincidence, this."

Marie grimaced as she tried to remember her line…and drew a complete blank. Fine. So she wouldn't be able to lie. The word wasn't even a part of her vocabulary anyway. She opened her mouth to tell him she knew everything when Ian cleared his throat.

"I told her what's going on, Frank."

Marie stared at him as if he'd gone soft in the head just as her excuse for being there popped into her own head. Dry cleaning. She'd come by to drop off her dry cleaning. A perfectly plausible excuse.

A lie.

Her father started turning toward Ian. Marie grabbed his arms and forced him to look at her. "I made him tell me, Papa. I knew something was going on, that you were in some sort of trouble, and since I couldn't get anything from you or Mama, I went to the next best source."

Her uncle Gino tsked-tsked behind her. "Sounds like a violation of attorney-client privilege to me, Frankie—you know, if you ask me."

"Yeah, well, he wasn't askin' you," Vinnie said.

Gino shrugged. "Just thought he should know. You know, in case he didn't already."

Marie watched Ian round her father to exit the office, then take a couple steps back. "This isn't a traffic violation, Frank," he said, holding his hands up as if to indicate he didn't hold any weapons. He uneasily glanced over at the men sitting at the table behind him. "Don't you think your family has a right to know?"

"My family does know."

Marie stared at her father, rendered completely dumbstruck. "I didn't know."

"Your mother knows. So do your brothers."

Her grip on his arms slipped as she blinked at him. "So what does that mean? That I'm not family?"

He blew out a long breath. "That's not what I'm saying at all. I'm saying that I didn't want you worried. Hell, girl, I knew you'd jump right in the middle of all this like a she-wolf protecting her pack. You know, seeing as you're a lawyer and all."

"You're damn right I would have."

He held up his finger. "That's why I didn't want you to be told."

The large room went dead silent.

Marie didn't know what to say. Not about his not

wanting her to know anything, but finding out that
everyone else in her family but her had known.

Ian cleared his throat. "Look, who knew about it
and who didn't is really a nonissue now, wouldn't you
say? So why don't we just take a look at the situation
as it stands?"

Marie straightened her shoulders. "I'm representing
my father."

"The hell you are," Frankie Sr. said, staring at her.

Ian heaved a sigh. "Before this…meeting degener-
ates any more than it already has, let's say that Marie…sits in as cocounsel."

Her father narrowed his eyes at Ian. "What's that?"

Gino rocked back in his chair. "It means she can sit
in on the meetings, be privy to everything happening,
and can help out, but when the money's on the table,
your man Ian is in charge."

Ian grinned. "Very well put."

MARIE WATCHED HER UNCLE Vinnie hit Gino in the
arm. "What makes you so knowledgeable in the legal
arena?"

Gino smoothed down the front of his shirt. "Back
in the old days I once fancied myself an attorney."

Uncle Vinnie chuckled. "Back in the old days he
was arrested for impersonating an attorney."

Marie would have laughed at the shocked expression
on Ian's face but she was in the middle of frying her
own fish. "I want to take over, period, Papa. I'm more
than capable—"

"I like Ian's idea better." He tapped a meaty finger
against Ian's chest. "You be the attorney." He pointed
at her. "You help him."

"But—"

"No buts."

And just like that the discussion was over. Marie was forced to "button her lip," as her father had once been fond of telling her, and respect his wishes.

"What's say we get those books," Ian said, leading the way into the office.

Marie stayed put as her father followed him, blindly staring at their backs. As the sting from his exclusion abated, and the reality of the situation settled in, she started to feel...relieved.

She was in.

Yes, she should have been in from the beginning, but this was a definite step in the right direction. Progress. And while she had just won this small battle, it was a minor victory as far as the war was concerned. Essentially she was being presented with a chance to finally prove once and for all to her father and the rest of her family that she was capable of not only taking care of herself, but them as well.

She knew a moment of hesitation. But while she was confident in her career as an attorney, representing someone who used to change your diapers was more than a tad off-putting. No, she might not be as sharp as Dulcy, or as brassy as Jena, but if she could not only survive the Bertelli family, including her three lughead brothers, but become a success in her own right, then she was up for anything.

And now was the perfect time to prove that.

SHE WAS GOING TO GET THEM all arrested.

Ian stood up to act as a human barrier between Marie and one of the two U.S. Treasury agents, John Roberts. "Whoa, whoa, whoa. I think we all could use a bit of a time-out here."

Marie's blue eyes flashed. And damn if, despite their present circumstances, Ian thought she was the most beautiful woman he'd ever laid eyes on.

She focused her attention on Ian. "I think Mr. Roberts and his buddy here need to have their heads examined."

Essentially the worst that Ian had predicted might happen was happening.

Marie had accompanied him and Frankie Sr. into the meeting room at Treasury headquarters, and every word either of the agents said from there on out Marie had taken very personally. Mainly because they did know about the car sitting at the local dump and the reason why the junkyard manager hadn't known anything about any treasury agents was that the agents had gotten to the car before it had been towed there.

So what it boiled down to was that Frankie Bertelli Sr. wasn't only being investigated for money laundering...but it was a pretty safe bet that murder was also somewhere on the list. Might even be number one. Establish motive first by getting Frankie to admit he was upset with his bookkeeper. Have him spill his frustration with him and possibly even get him to admit that, yes, at some point in their thirty-five-year working relationship he may have uttered words along the lines of "'do that and I'll kill,'" no matter the context. And before you knew it, Frankie Sr. would have a new piece of jewelry in the form of handcuffs.

He glanced toward the two-way mirror. He didn't have to wonder if they were being videotaped. He knew it. And he had no doubt that someone in the district attorney's office, if not the D.A. himself, was either behind that glass or would be the recipient of the videotape should Frank give the agents what they wanted.

And given Marie's emotional state, she might just unwittingly hand them that.

He sighed and dry-washed his face with his hands. "Look, what's say we all take five, okay? I don't know about you, but I could use a cold beverage right about now." He looked at Roberts, filled with the desire to punch the guy right in the mouth himself, but maintaining a professional distance that allowed him to recognize that wasn't such a good idea. "Do you know where I can find one?"

The agent pointed toward the door. "Hang a left. There's a machine at the end of the hall."

"Okay, we'll take five," the other agent said, opening a door at the opposite end of the room that presumably led to their offices. "Come on," he said to Roberts.

And just like that Ian, Marie and Frankie Sr. were alone.

Ian looked at Frank.

He had to give the old guy credit. Not once had he lost his temper over the past three meetings with the agents. Hadn't batted an eye at one single question.

He looked at Marie.

Now she, on the other hand, hadn't been in the room three minutes before she was on her feet reaming the agents for their incompetence.

Frankie shook his head as he stared at where the agents had been moments before. "I knew we shouldn't have brought her. But no. You had to suggest she be cocounsel." He leaned back and looked at Ian. "And here I thought that meant she was going to be a secretary or something. You know, take notes."

Marie made a sound of frustration.

"Come on." Ian took her arm. "Let's go get that soda." He opened the door. "Frankie, you want something?"

"Yeah. Bring me one of those tonic waters if they got 'em."

Marie stared at her father with her mouth slightly agape, then led the way from the room.

Ian could have sworn he heard her say "tonic water" under her breath but that didn't make any sense so he didn't pursue it.

Instead, he said, "You know you're about an insult away from getting your father arrested and us booked as accessories, don't you?"

She was walking so fast even he had to hurry to keep up with her, which was saying a lot considering he had at least a foot on her. "They're both lucky I don't take a contract out on both their stupid carcasses," she replied.

Ian slowed his step as he stared at her, then stopped altogether. He watched as she did much the same thing, her back to him. Then she turned, the expression of shock on her face so thorough Ian allowed himself to feel relieved.

"I can't believe I just said that," she whispered.

At once, all the fight seemed to seep out of her. Her shoulders sagged and she didn't so much lean against the wall as she appeared to need it for support. "Why didn't you tell me this was so serious?"

Ian leaned a shoulder against the opposite wall and crossed his arms, deciding it best to say nothing.

"I thought...I thought this was just some run-of-the-mill inquiry. You know, your tax returns looked a little fishy so we want you to clarify everything for us." She looked at him, her heart very nearly beating right there in her eyes. "They're seriously considering arresting him for money laundering."

Ian watched an employee step around them, get a cola, then make his way back down the hall again. He didn't have to point out to her that if it had been a matter of a simple tax discrepancy they would be dealing with I.R.S. agents and not treasury agents. He knew she was talking her way around the situation in order to regain a hold on it.

Marie made a sound suspiciously like a laugh. "My father the dry cleaner is a money launderer. Sounds like the title of a really bad 'B' movie."

Ian cracked a soft smile. She met his gaze and held it for a long moment.

"They think he killed Nunzio, don't they?"

Ian's smile vanished and he looked down at his shoes.

She held up her hands. "No, wait, don't answer that. Because I don't think I could bear it if you said yes." She briefly closed her eyes. "God, this is like some kind of nightmare, you know? Like I was plucked from *The Brady Bunch* and plopped down in the middle of *The Godfather*." She swallowed hard. "Okay, maybe not *The Brady Bunch*, but you know what I mean."

He did.

"You don't think I should go back in there, do you?" she whispered, then opened her eyes to gaze at him.

He slowly shook his head.

She covered her face with her hands, then sighed as she dropped her arms to her sides. "You're right. I'm too close to this to be of any real help."

Ian hiked a brow.

"Oh, shut up."

Funny, but he didn't think he'd said a single word over the past couple of minutes. She had done all the talking. And had come to exactly the conclusion she would have rejected had *he* suggested she walk away from the meeting.

"Okay. I'll leave." She pushed from the wall and pointed a finger at him in much the same way her father had back at the cleaners. "But you take care of him, you hear me?" She curved her finger under one of the buttons of his shirt and absently ran the back against his chest. "I'll be waiting at my office to hear from you."

He smiled at her as he tucked her sexy, curly red hair behind her ear. "Same time tonight?"

She smiled back, then nodded.

Ian watched as she stepped down the hall, collected her things from the meeting room and presumably said goodbye to her father. Then she waggled her fingers at Ian as she disappeared down the hall.

He shook his head and got one soda and one tonic water from the machine before heading back to the meeting.

This man-woman stuff boggled the mind. Complicated. But once you had the hang of it, it was workable.

He stepped through the door to find the agents entering the other side of the room. "Okay, guys, let's get down to business. What do I have to do to get you to close my client's case?"

9

THERE DIDN'T SEEM TO BE enough air in the room. Marie fought for breath as she rolled off Ian's sweat-drenched body and collapsed against the silk sheets. How could she feel exhilarated, exhausted, on fire and satisfied all at once?

Ian sounded winded as he chuckled softly next to her. "I keep thinking things can't possibly get better. Then—bam!—you prove me wrong again."

Marie smiled. "I was just going to say the same thing about you."

He turned his head to look at her, his dark hair tousled and damp against his forehead. "You were not."

"I was, too."

She tried to swallow at the same time she was catching her breath and nearly choked. She rolled over onto her stomach and hung her head over the side of the bed. "I can't seem to catch my breath. And my heart's beating so hard if we hadn't just finished I'd swear I was having a heart attack."

She felt his hand on her bare bottom.

She looked over her shoulder at him through the curtain of her hair. "Haven't you had enough?"

"Mmm." He glanced at his watch. "For at least the next five minutes."

Marie glanced at the clock on the stand. After midnight.

"God."

She started to rouse herself, but Ian stayed her with a hand on the back of her thigh. "Where do you think you're going?"

"Home," she said, lethargically reaching for her jeans where they lay on the floor.

"Home," he repeated.

She nodded. "Yeah. Frankie Jr. was waiting up for me when I got home last night. I swear I suffered through the inquisition."

She got her snug jeans as far up as they were going to go without standing. Or...

She lay back, her head against Ian's hard abdomen as she pulled her jeans up the rest of the way. Only when it was time to get up again, she couldn't.

Ian brushed her hair back from her face. "When's he going back to his wife, anyway?"

She grimaced as she stared at the ceiling, content to listen to the sound of Ian's pounding heart under her head. "I don't know. It's starting to look like never." She tilted her head to look at him. "I threatened to tell Mom about his situation last night. Want to talk about your heart attacks." She smiled to herself, remembering her brother's startled expression.

Marie budged her hand up until she could tuck it under the crisp hair of Ian's calf where she let it lie. "I stopped by the construction company today."

"Frankie Jr.'s?"

"Uh-huh." She was happy that her breathing was finally returning to normal—and shocked by the desire to turn her head and coax Ian's erection back to life. "I'm pretty fed up with the lack of activity on my brother's part. So I decided I needed to get a look at this Lola person."

Ian grinned at her. "There you go again. Jumping into the fray."

She grimaced. "Yes, well, I figure I had to unload all the frustration built up this afternoon at the Treasury Department."

"Mmm." He toyed with the snap on her jeans. "What's she look like?"

"Who?"

"Lola."

"Ah, you mean the homewrecker." She shifted her head to stare at the ceiling again. "I don't know. Pretty, I guess. But she didn't look anything like I expected her to, you know?"

He didn't say anything.

"It wasn't like her clothes were tight or her cleavage was hanging out. To hear my brother talk, you would think she walked around in a G-string all day."

"G-string. Mmm."

Marie swatted playfully at his arm. "Anyway, I found her...nice. I mean, you can see where she was probably a good stripper. But Frankie Jr.'s right. She seems to be a really good secretary."

"But is keeping her there worth the loss of your brother's family?"

Marie didn't know how to respond to that one. A few days ago she would have answered unequivocally no. But now that she had met Lola....

"Frankie saw his boys last night. Took them to dinner."

"That's good."

Marie shrugged her shoulders. "I suppose on the surface it looks that way. But there's only so much you can do with a one- and a two-year-old, you know?"

"Why didn't he take them to your mother's?"

Marie looked at him pointedly, an idea taking root in her mind.

"Oh, yeah, I forgot. She doesn't know Frankie Jr.'s living with you." He slid his finger into the waistband of her jeans, making her catch her breath. "You know, there's a really simple way of fixing that..."

"You know, I was just thinking the same thing. Not about telling my mother—what, do you want to see World War Three? But about Toni meeting Lola."

"She hasn't met her yet?"

"Uh-uh. She doesn't get out of the house much what with the kids and everything, you know? Besides, Frankie Jr. doesn't like her stopping by the office." She waved a hand. "That goes back way before Lola. He says she distracts him."

"And Lola doesn't?"

She glanced at him. "Actually from what I saw to-day...no, she doesn't distract any of them anymore. Sure, she's blond. She's attractive. But she doesn't take any guff from the guys there and they seem to respect her for that."

"Interesting."

"Isn't it just?"

She lay there for a long moment thinking about the situation and about how she could get her brother out of her apartment.

Ian took a deep breath. "Speaking of secretaries, have you had any luck getting someone in to replace yours?"

"Yes, actually. I mean after the first two disasters. The first temp didn't even know how to type and the second one jumped every time the phone rang and didn't come back after lunch hour. But Josephine…well, she's no Mona, but she's good." She sighed. "At least I can find everything again."

"Always a good thing."

She closed her eyes and hummed her agreement, just then realizing she was methodically rubbing her head back and forth against his stomach.

"Um, Marie?"

"Uh-huh?"

"I think you better stop that or else risk waking someone up."

She laughed softly as she swiveled her head to look at him. She moved her head a little farther south and found out that it was a little too late—he was already awake. "Oh?" she asked with mock innocence. "Are you hiding someone under the bed?"

Within a blink of an eye he had her pinned to the bed and was nudging her jean-covered legs apart with his knee. "You really didn't want to talk to your brother tonight anyway, did you?"

She lazily linked her arms around his neck. "Why? What else did you have in mind?"

He slowly, tantalizingly and very skillfully set out to show her…

THE FOLLOWING DAY Marie motioned the waiter to her table to take her and her friends' lunch order at a downtown restaurant.

"I told you she wouldn't come," Jena said, sighing and picking up her menu again.

Dulcy took a sip of water. "Granted, it was a long shot."

Marie grimaced as the waiter held up a finger asking her to wait a minute. She wasn't really sure what had compelled her to call Mona that morning at her new place of employment and invite her to lunch, but she did know she was disappointed their ex-secretary hadn't shown up. "Maybe she's running late."

Both of her friends looked at her over their menus.

"Okay, okay. So she stood me up." She glanced toward the door. "Maybe she came, saw the two of you with me and ran in the other direction."

Jena apparently made her selection then put her menu down. "Not likely. I think she would have joined us if she made it as far as the restaurant."

Dulcy's gaze followed someone. "Don't look now, but she's made it this far and looks like she's going all the way."

Marie nearly knocked over her water glass as she hurried to stand up.

Mona Lyndell was making her way toward their table. Marie's eyes widened as she noted the differences in the fifty-something woman. Sure, on Jena's advice she'd changed her hairstyle a couple months ago, and updated her glasses. But this...

"Wow," Dulcy summed up Marie's thoughts as she greeted the other woman with a brief hug, then stepped aside to allow Jena and Marie to do the same.

Mona took the seat between Marie and Jena. Jena couldn't seem to get over the transformation as she continued to stare at their guest. "Jesus, Mona, you look...well, damn hot."

A familiar side of Mona surfaced as color brushed her cheeks. "I haven't heard it put exactly that way, but thank you."

Dulcy pointed a finger at her rich cream-colored jacket. "Donna Karan, right?"

Mona nodded as she looked down at her clothes. "I

think that's what my personal shopping assistant told me.''

Jena's eyes widened. "Personal shopping assistant?" She groaned. "I've always wanted to consult one of those.''

"You don't need one, Jena. You shop okay on your own," Dulcy said.

Jena made a face. "Just the same. It has a nice ring to it, doesn't it? My personal shopping assistant.''

Marie cleared her throat and concentrated on the reason they were all gathered for lunch. "You're doing well then, Mona?''

Mona's handsome face brightened as she smiled. "Oh, very. I think the change in scenery did me loads of good. Made me take a good long look at my life, so to speak.'' She leaned forward and her voice dropped to a whisper. "I'm even dating.''

The three women looked at each other.

Jena was the one to say what they were thinking. "But you have been dating. Barry.''

Mona lifted her brows. "Had I? I couldn't be sure. I thought all we were doing was having sex.''

Marie spewed water all over the table. All three of the other women laughed as Mona and Dulcy helped mop up the mess.

"I'm sorry," she said, looking at her friends from under her lashes. "I just hadn't expected you to put it exactly that way, Mona, if I can borrow your own words.''

"A month ago I would never have dreamed of saying something like that," the older woman admitted. "But that good long look I talked about has made me realize some things.''

"About Barry?" Dulcy asked.

"About myself."

The waiter finally stepped up. "Good, we're all here then. What'll you have?"

He looked at Mona first while Marie muttered under her breath, "A big helping of sanity all around, please."

Dulcy smiled next to her.

When the waiter finally left them, Mona continued. "I mean, can you believe I wasted nearly thirty years of my life waiting for Barry to notice me? Through three marriages..." She drifted off, her gaze glued to the tablecloth. "Well, maybe only through the last two. His first wife...well, he loved her. To distraction. I think that's part of why I felt the way I did about him. No matter how bad it got...he stuck it out with her. Stayed with her. Nursed her." She shook her head, her voice growing lower as she spoke. "When she died, I was afraid he was going to go with her."

Marie looked at Dulcy.

"Barry's wife had cancer," Dulcy explained.

"Is that what she died of?"

"No." Dulcy shook her head. "She took her own life when things got bad at the end."

Marie's eyes widened.

Mona added sugar substitute to her iced tea. "God, how he loved her. And I thought any man that can love a woman that much is a good man."

Silence reigned over the table. Marie hadn't known that about Barry. Then again, that wasn't exactly the type of information you shared around the water cooler. It was too serious...too sad...too personal.

Marie followed Mona's lead and reached for the sugar substitute, then changed her mind and reached for the sugar. She chose to ignore the looks of interest her friends gave her. Okay, so she never went for the real thing. But they didn't have to make a federal case out of it. The truth was, she'd lost five pounds over the past week, even though she'd been eating far more than she usually did.

She shifted in her chair. Wild, satisfying sex must burn more calories than she'd ever imagined.

Jena buttered a roll, then wiped her fingers on her napkin. "So what happened between you and Barry then?" She took a bite of the bread. "I mean, after the great sex?"

Mona glanced at her, then smiled. "I didn't say it was great."

"You didn't say it wasn't."

"Mmm. You're right." She leaned back as the waiter put her salad in front of her. "He refused to come out of the closet."

This time Dulcy nearly spewed her water all over the table.

"Everything all right, ma'am?" the waiter asked Dulcy as he placed a salad in front of her, then Jena.

Jena gaped at Mona. "Barry's gay?"

"Heavens no! I was speaking in terms of our relationship. To bring our relationship out of the closet."

Marie removed the hand she had smacked over her heart.

Dulcy stared at Marie. "Did the waiter just call me ma'am?"

Marie nodded. "Yes, he did."

Jena rolled her eyes. "You're five months pregnant, Dulcy, with a rock the size of Gibraltar on your finger. What do you want him to call you?"

"Miss until I indicate otherwise. Which might be

never." Dulcy grimaced. "He just lost two percent of his tip."

All of them laughed, including Dulcy.

Jena turned back to Mona. "So you and Barry haven't actually been out on a real date then?"

Mona shook her head. "No dinner. No late-night phone calls. Not even coffee." She speared her salad with fervor, making Marie wince. "Things would either just spontaneously happen at the office, or he'd show up on my doorstep and things would go from there." She gave a wry smile. "One night when we were...um, when I dropped something in my apartment the neighbor came over to make sure everything was all right. When I went back into the bedroom, I found Barry hanging from my window gauging the fifteen-foot jump." She sighed. "He was so desperate not to be seen there with me, he nearly broke his neck trying to get out."

They all thought about that one a minute as something in Marie's head clicked.

"Mona?" Dulcy said quietly. "Did you ever think that Barry might have been trying to protect your virtue?"

"Then why didn't he ever invite me out to dinner? Take me to a movie? Bring me a flower he had taken from a neighbor's garden? Anything to indicate that I was more than a...well, that I meant more to him?"

"Maybe his attraction for you wouldn't allow for clear thoughts."

"Or maybe he was ashamed of me." She carefully put her fork down, then slowly reached for her water. "That's the only way I can figure it, Dulcy. I've thought about this for hours on end. For weeks. He flaunted all of his previous affairs—all stylish, attractive women, the type you show off. Take your almost mother-in-law Beatrix Wheeler, for example.''

Dulcy made a face. "No, please, you keep her."

Mona didn't respond to the comment. "All of us knew Barry was...what's the phrase you all use? Oh, yes. Doing her.''

Marie's eyes bulged, but Mona continued without having noticed. "He made no secret of his affair with Trixie. In fact, he seemed to relish letting everyone know he was...doing her.''

The waiter brought Marie's appetizer, a double order of fried mozzarella sticks. For the second time her friends stared at her.

"What?" she practically barked. "It's cheese."

"It's fried cheese," Jena said, clearly in shock. "I've never seen you eat fried cheese."

"Then you haven't been paying close attention."

Dulcy pointed her fork at her as she swallowed a bite of her salad. "No, Marie, Miss I'll-only-have-a-salad-I'll-only-eat-half-of. You've never ordered fried cheese. Something's definitely up."

Marie smiled at her. "Then it's a good thing I'm not the topic of discussion today then, isn't it?"

"Speaking of which," Jena said, turning back to Mona.

Marie inwardly sagged in relief. She and Ian, well...

She put down the mozzarella stick she had halfway to her mouth. She and Ian what? She felt something click loudly in her head.

"What would it take for you to come back to Lomax, Ferris, McCade and Bertelli, Mona?" Jena brushed breadcrumbs from her hands. "Name it and you've got it."

Mona began shaking her head before Jena even finished. "I'm not coming back."

Dulcy gave an exaggerated groan, then sat back. "Please don't say that. The place is not the same without you there, Mona. You're like family."

Mona met her gaze, the shadow in her eyes making even Marie hurt. "I can't, Dulcy. This has nothing to do with any of you. You're all good girls." She smiled. "And I miss you, too. It's just that…I can't work day in and day with Barry anymore. It causes me too much pain." She swallowed hard. "It hurts to even think about him."

Under her breath Jena muttered a long line of what could only be curse words, then smiled at everyone as if she hadn't said anything. "And if we get rid of Barry?"

"Jena! We can't do that," Dulcy gasped. "You forget, the firm was originally his."

Jena frowned. "There is that. But I'm sure that in a court of law…"

"You wouldn't dare!"

Mona held up her hand. "No one's suing anybody. I'm not coming back to the firm. I'm flattered that you girls would even go to this extent to try to entice me back. I appreciate the gesture, really. You made me feel more wanted than I've felt in twenty-five years. But I can't come back. End of story. Period. Bold. Double underline."

The table went silent again.

Marie quietly chewed a bite of cheese, mulling over everything that had been said, and a lot more that hadn't been said.

Then the reason for the click she'd heard in her head earlier dawned on her. Essentially her and Ian's relationship was being carried out under cover, both figuratively and literally. And while that had been okay with her twenty minutes ago, suddenly it wasn't all right anymore.

She covertly eyed Mona. Is that where she'd be in twenty-five years? Okay, so she and Ian didn't work in the same office, but the parallels between the two relationships made her itch.

So then where did that leave them?

"Marie?" Jena waved her hand to catch her attention.

Marie blinked at her. "What?"

"I've been trying to get your attention for a full minute. What's the matter? Did you fall into a food-induced coma?"

"Very funny."

Dulcy cleared her throat. "We were just saying that we'd like Mona to attend my baby shower at the firm next Friday."

Marie squinted at her and opened her mouth. The only baby shower she knew of was the one Esmerelda was throwing for Dulcy next month out at the ranch. Dulcy stared at her in one of those warning, wink-wink kind of ways and Marie snapped her mouth shut again. She had no idea why, or what was going on, but she knew she should just go with the flow.

"Yes," she said, smiling at Mona who was eyeing them all a tad suspiciously. "That would be very nice." She reached out and touched her hand. "We'd love it if you could come, Mona."

"Barry's going out of town next week, so you won't have to worry about running into him," Jena added.

"Oh?"

Marie wished she could reach her friend to kick her

in the shin. Was she forgetting that up until last week Mona had been the one in charge of Barry's schedule?

Dulcy spoke up. "Yes. His cousin is scheduled for surgery in Manhattan then. He's going to visit her."

Mona nodded. "Janice." She shifted a couple times then eyed each of them in turn, making Marie wonder if it would have been better to keep the lying to a minimum. "Of course, I'll come," she finally said.

"Good," Jena said.

Marie sat through the remainder of the meal, feeling like Judas at the last supper. She wasn't sure what her friends had in mind, but she was pretty certain it would be something she wouldn't approve of.

Finally, the meal was over and Mona was gone, leaving Marie alone with Dulcy and Jena. But once she found out what they had in mind, she wished like hell she hadn't asked them to tell her.

"You can't do that!" Marie whispered harshly as she walked with her two friends out to their cars. "What you're proposing to do is...well, aside from being illegal," she strongly stressed the word. "It's wrong, wrong, wrong. And downright scheming."

Jena shrugged her shoulders. "Desperate times call for desperate measures."

Suddenly Marie thought the sentence fit her entire life perfectly.

10

IAN USED A POT HOLDER to take his nuked frozen dinner out of the microwave oven, then he stuck his fork in the leathery meat on his way back out to the living room. The smell of his roommate Tyler's aftershave wafted to him from the open bathroom door at the end of the hall. No doubt he was getting ready for another date with yet a different woman. The guy seemed to do little else as of late. And the two-bedroom condo seemed a little crowded what with the two of them and Tyler's endless dates bumping into each other every night. The apartment had seemed roomy when Ian first rented it upon his return from Chicago. And he supposed it still was. It boasted more square footage than some one-family homes and had airy balconies and a large living and dining room area. But he wished he had thought to get a place where the bedrooms weren't back to back. It was all he could do to get to sleep at night with all the noise Tyler and his girl de jour made.

Better the guy should be looking for a job, Ian thought, so he could boot him out without it weighing on his conscience.

As it was, Ian couldn't even relax in his own apartment because Tyler blamed poverty on his inability to take his dates out anywhere, so he had to invite them there. Which would be fine if the moron didn't have a date every night of the week. Ian swore that, rather than looking for work, Tyler combed the nearby supermarkets, cafés and department stores picking up women.

It was just after six. Three hours to go before he would meet his own woman in Room 7. He flicked on the local evening news, then wished he hadn't. The first image to pop up onto the screen was of his own mug, the footage taken when he had led Frankie Sr. from the front doors of the U.S. Treasury Department earlier that afternoon.

He put his unappetizing dinner down on the coffee table and groaned. Loudly.

"Don't you think this is a little premature, Connie?" his taped image said to the on-the-spot reporter who had asked him to comment on the ongoing investigation and Frankie's guilt or innocence. *"Mr. Bertelli hasn't even been charged with a crime."*

Yet.

He hadn't said the word, but there it hung anyway.

Ian stretched his neck and took a deep breath. Oh, he was familiar with the tactics. Knew they came out of the law enforcement handbook on how to bag a crook and suspected the U.S. Treasury agents had copies tucked under their bed pillows. Step one, let the target know you're on to them and hope they trip up and give up the evidence you need. Step two, try to force said target into giving you the evidence you need by subjecting him to intense questioning.

And here was step three. Leak news bites to the local media and turn the noncase into a case in the court of public opinion.

He grimaced. He only hadn't realized they would move on to step three so quickly. Had he known, he would have saved Frankie Sr. the embarrassment of being bombarded by furry microphones and accusatory questions while the cameras were rolling, and he would have snuck him out of the back of the building instead.

Ian supposed he should be thankful Marie had left the Treasury Department long before that. He could only imagine what her response to the reporters would have been. There probably would have been a lot of bleeping when the footage was aired.

"Hey, isn't that you?" Tyler said, coming up from behind him clad in only a towel—one of Ian's—and rubbing his hair with another—again, Ian's.

"Yeah." He reached to shut off the television.

"No, don't. I want to see the weather. I'm going skiing this weekend and want to make sure there's going to be some good packed snow."

Skiing. Great. Tyler had only been able to make half of his half of the rent this month, but he could afford to go skiing.

But Ian didn't say anything. He already knew he'd hear an endless stream of excuses. He picked up his dinner again. Tyler would probably tell him the arrangements had been made months ago, before he'd been laid off, and the deposit was nonrefundable, so, hey, what was a guy to do? He took a frustrated bite of his glorified Salisbury steak. A guy should kick his deadbeat roommate out on his butt, that's what.

Tyler sat down on the arm of the black leather sofa. "Damn. That place is toast, man."

Ian looked up, relieved to see that the news had moved on to another story. He forked some dry noodles into his mouth as he watched bright yellow flames devour a one-story building. He squinted at the image, the hair on the back of his neck rising. It looked familiar...

"Hey, it's the Shady Pines Motel," Tyler said unnecessarily as the camera angle widened to include the on-the-spot reporter standing next to the neon sign announcing the same.

The noodles nearly took up permanent resident in Ian's throat. Instead he reached for his glass of water and used the entire contents to help the tasteless food go down.

Tyler crossed his arms and grinned. "I've had some good times in that motel, man. You know, way back when. Hey, where're you going?"

Ian barely heard him as he strode to the kitchen, closed the swinging door and picked up the phone.

"NOT ENOUGH GARLIC. Cut some more."

Marie's hands stilled where she was chopping up garlic cloves on a wooden cutting board. She eyed the butcher knife she held, then moved it so the overhead light glinted off the honed steel.

Next to her Frankie Jr. held up his hands. "Whoa. I know that look. Toni gives it to me all the time."

"Oh?" Marie said, holding up the knife and smiling at him.

"Uh-huh. It means I'm five seconds away from ending up on the cutting board myself."

Marie sighed and put the knife into the sink. "That's not the type of 'oh' it was. What I meant was 'oh, I'm surprised you even remember what your wife looks like, much less which expressions she used to wear.'"

Frankie Jr. blinked at her. "What do you mean? I see her every day."

"When you go see the kids." Marie transferred the garlic from the board to join the chopped onion already in the heated olive oil in the pan on the stove. "Have you talked to her lately, Frankie? I mean, about the situation? When you might be going home?''

Frankie crossed his arms over his chest. ''We don't say much. Five words, maybe. She tells me what the kids did that day. I ask if she needs anything. I hand over the money and we say good-night.''

Marie held up a finger. ''Healthy relationship, that.''

''Yeah, well, what do you want me to say?''

''Oh, I don't know. How about, 'I love you, Toni, and I want to come home because I miss you and the kids and our family.'''

''She'd never buy it.''

Marie stared at him. ''Why? Because it's not true?''

''No, because it's not something I'd say.''

She stirred the garlic and onion. ''Yes, well, maybe this is the time to start saying it.''

Frankie leaned against the refrigerator and grinned at her. ''What's the matter, sis? Am I cramping your style or something?''

Marie pulled the refrigerator open, forcing him to move. ''No, but you are driving me insane. Every night I come home there you are, sitting in front of the TV waiting for me to fix dinner for you.''

He shrugged. ''You'd be fixing for yourself anyway.''

Marie eyed the knife again. ''I work, you work. Would it kill you to put something together every once in a while?''

''I don't know how to cook.''

''Really? Is that why you're always in here telling me how to do it then?''

He grimaced. ''Ouch.''

''The truth hurts.''

''You can say that again.''

The only sounds in the room for the next couple of minutes were of Marie putting water on to boil and adding fresh tomato to the onion and garlic, and of the evening news on in the other room. She was aware of Frankie's gaze on her every move and could tell he was biting his tongue not to tell her how to do something.

As was par for the course, the instant she got home Frankie Jr. asked how everything was going with their father's case. She'd fill him in, he'd nod, get that thoughtful look on his face that mirrored both worry and the certainty that everything would work out okay, then he'd move on to other things. Like criticism over her cooking.

"Hey, sis, mind if I ask you a question?"

"Never stopped you before."

"Cute. Real cute." He leaned against the opposite counter, making Marie wonder what it was about men and leaning. Did they feel that's what the items were put there for, to lean on? Or were they just too damn lazy to hold themselves upright?

"So?" she asked. "What's your question?"

"Where do you go every night?"

Marie's throat tightened. He had to ask, didn't he?

"I mean, you don't get any phone calls from guys or anything. And I'm pretty sure that it's a guy you sneak out of here every night to meet." He stiffened slightly. "At least I hope it's a guy, you know, and not…"

Marie didn't bite. She was too preoccupied with how he'd phrased his comment. He hadn't said "date" or "go out with" he'd said "meet."

Which, of course, was exactly what she had been

doing. Meeting Ian in Room 7 at the Shady Pines Motel on the outskirts of town.

"I don't sneak."

"No, maybe not. But you do take off around nine and don't come back until after midnight. One night you didn't come home at all."

She was surprised he'd noticed, seeing as his eyelids impeded his vision while he snored.

She glanced at him. "You ever think I just go out by myself? That I need to get away from you for a while?"

He grinned. "Never."

She made a face.

The cordless perched on the wall behind him rang. Marie immediately hurried to pick it up but he laid a hand on it first.

"It might be Ma," she reminded him.

He shook his head and knocked a knuckle against the caller ID display box. "Not unless she's calling from somewhere else, and Ma's nowhere but home this time of night."

He picked up the handheld as Marie watched nervously.

Oh, for Pete's sake, Ian never called her here. Why should he start now? She forced herself to return to her cooking and pretend she didn't care one way or another who Frank might talk to. She was mighty thankful that she hadn't programmed his name into the caller box though.

"May I ask who's calling, please?" Frankie Jr. said with a stern but polite voice.

The tiny hairs on the back of Marie's neck stood on end.

"What, you don't have a name?"

Marie marched to stand in front of her brother and held her hand out. "Give it to me."

"Just a sec," he said into the phone. He held it up out of her reach for a moment. "He says he's a colleague from work."

She glared at him.

"Funny he wouldn't give his name, though."

"Frankie..." she said in warning.

"Tell me who it is, Marie."

She whacked him in the stomach, then grabbed the extension when he flinched.

Frankie grinned. "I'll find out."

"Just shut up and watch the sauce."

Marie hurried into the other room, then put the phone to her ear.

"Did I cause trouble?" Ian's voice filled her ear.

"Nothing I can't handle," she said.

Talking to him filled her with excitement and dread at the same time. Excitement because that's always how she felt when she spoke to him. Dread because whatever he had to say couldn't be good.

She turned to find Frankie Jr. standing in the kitchen doorway openly listening in.

She stalked across the room and closed the door on him, listening as he cursed on the other side when she caught him in the knee.

"What is it?" she asked quietly. "It's not... something hasn't happened to my father, has it? Has he been arrested?"

"No, no, nothing as serious as that."

"Then what?"

"We can't meet tonight."

Marie slid down to sit in an old wooden rocker her mother had given her when she moved out.

"Why?" she forced herself to ask when a little part of her just wanted to say "sure, okay, no big deal" and hang up.

"Are you watching the news?"

"No..."

"Switch it on."

"It's on, I just wasn't watching it."

There was a heartbeat of a pause as she stared at the television screen, then Ian said, "We can't meet tonight because there's no longer anyplace for us to meet."

Marie stared at the little box above the right shoulder of the newscaster depicting a burning building, then listened as she said that the cause of the fire at the Shady Pines Motel had yet to be determined, but that arson was suspected.

"Oh, God," Marie said, thinking back to the night before. All the candles. Had they inadvertently left one burning? Or had a spark from one of them smoldered until it had ignited into a full-blown blaze?

"Probably a drunk smoker," Ian said, as if reading her thoughts and trying to allay her fears.

"Yeah, probably," she said, biting her bottom lip.

"At least no one was hurt. The report said everyone got out and that only the motel manager had suffered some smoke inhalation from where he'd fallen asleep in his chair behind the counter."

"That's good. I mean, that no one was hurt."

She could practically hear him smile. "I knew what you meant."

She smiled back. "I know."

Silence stretched as Marie absorbed the impact of the news.

"What are the chances of you getting Frankie Jr. to move out tonight?" Ian finally murmured into her ear.

"Short of forcing him to leave at gunpoint? Between slim and none."

He sighed and lowered his voice as if someone could hear him on his end. "My roommate's staying in, too."

Marie thought about suggesting they meet somewhere else, but nothing that came to mind seemed appealing. Did they upgrade to a hotel? One with a properly working toilet and an up-to-date sprinkler system?

She rested her head against her palm. No. Meeting in Room 7 was one thing. Meeting somewhere else…well, she didn't know why it didn't appeal to her just then, but it didn't.

"I don't suppose you would be interested in going—"

"No."

"Didn't think so."

Marie swallowed. "Well, thanks for calling, I guess."

"Yeah. Don't mention it."

Why was she all of a sudden at a loss for words?

"I'll call you tomorrow at work?" he asked.

"Yeah. Tomorrow."

A pause. "Good night, Marie."

She saw the kitchen door slightly inch open and caught sight of Frankie trying to hear her. "Good night."

She pulled the phone from her ear and pushed the disconnect button, suppressing the desire to throw the phone at her brother.

"The sauce done?" she asked.

Frankie opened the door the rest of the way and grinned at her. "What? Tonight off?"

She stared at the phone in her hand. ''Yes. Something like that.''

She moved to put the cordless down on the old leather chest that doubled as a coffee table when it rang again.

She nearly leapt out of the rocker.

''Hello?'' she said.

''My place. Eleven. Don't knock. I'll be waiting.''

Marie smiled so wide her face muscles hurt. She didn't even get a chance to respond before Ian hung up.

Frankie frowned. ''On again.''

Marie pushed from the chair. ''Oh, be quiet and feed me, will you? I'm going to need a lot of energy.''

''For what?'' Frankie asked as she ducked under his arm into the kitchen. ''Oh, Marie. I'm shocked.''

She blinked at him innocently. ''Why? I only meant that I need energy to try to help you figure out how to get back into your house.''

She could tell by his grimace that he knew that's not what she meant. But right that minute she was too happy to care. She was going to Ian's place tonight.

A FEW HOURS LATER Marie stood outside Ian's second-floor condo adjusting and readjusting her skirt. Why she'd worn the stupid thing was beyond her. She'd never given much thought to her appearance when she'd snuck out to meet Ian before this.

But tonight she'd gone all out. Snug skirt. Clingy blouse. Heels. And even panty hose that she usually wore only to work.

She supposed the extra attention might have something to do with Frankie Jr. admitting that he knew she was seeing someone. Or, more specifically, *meeting* someone. Not that she thought she was fooling him before when she ducked out of her apartment at the same time every night, but at least she'd kept up the appearance of propriety.

Tonight her brother had given a low wolf whistle when she'd emerged from her bedroom all dolled up.

"I hope this idiot appreciates you for who you are, sis," he said, moving to put her in a headlock.

She'd evaded him, then told him how much his easy-going reaction surprised her. No threats to tell their mother. No further attempts to learn who she was seeing. No speeches on the importance of protection.

He'd shrugged. "I'm the last one who should be judging anyone, you know? Besides, I owe you one for not telling Ma about me and Toni."

Now Marie nervously glanced at her watch and quelled the desire to knock—Ian had told her not to. What would Ma have to say when she found out that two out of her four children weren't exactly toeing the family line? She'd probably camp out at the Holy Rosary Catholic Church and not emerge until she'd burned every candle in the place.

She nervously shifted her weight from foot to foot. Okay, so she was early, but she felt stupid standing out in the hall like this. She glanced at the door of the other condo behind her.

The door to Ian's condo opened suddenly and she was hauled inside.

Marie gasped, blinking against the complete and utter darkness.

"Shh," Ian whispered against her ear. "It's just me."

Marie was confused. Had the electric gone out?

She didn't understand why all the lights were out. "But—"

Ian's hand curved down to her bottom, pressing her against him as his mouth claimed hers.

Desire swirled with confusion, making her strangely dizzy. She grabbed onto his shoulders to steady herself, the texture of his tongue against hers pushing all thought from her mind, replacing it with the sheer force of white-hot desire and need.

"Come on," he whispered, his breath coming in ragged gasps as he pulled his mouth from hers.

She licked her lips and looked around. An attempt at making the place more romantic? But there were no candles, no lights on at all. Maybe he didn't have any lamps? But surely there were ceiling fixtures. She shook her head slightly. It didn't make any sense.

The scent of leather caressed her nose along with some sort of air freshener she couldn't identify and the unique, manly smell of Ian as he walked in front of her.

He pulled her into a room and closed the door.

"God, when I thought I wouldn't be able to see you tonight, I went crazy." He reached for her.

Marie pressed her hands against his chest and pushed when he tried to kiss her again. "You're not really seeing me now, either."

She felt his gaze on her in the dark.

"The lights?" she whispered, wondering why she was whispering. Probably because he was. Which didn't make any sense either.

Ian sighed. "My roommate's in the next room."

Okay. That explained it. He didn't want to wake his roommate. That was thoughtful of him.

Bedsprings squeaked followed by what sounded like

a woman's low moan from the next room. Marie hiked a brow. Then again, maybe consideration had nothing to do with it. At least not consideration of the variety she'd originally thought.

She squinted, trying to make out Ian's features in the dim light filtering through the slats of his window blinds. "You're kidding me, right? I mean, there wasn't this much noise at the motel."

He skimmed his hands over her arms. "Unfortunately, the motel isn't an option anymore."

He kissed her long and hard, sending heat simmering through her veins and over her skin. She went boneless against him, her hands caressing rather than restraining, need swelling deep in her belly.

How was it possible that she could want him even more now than before? By all rights, she should have satisfied at least a fraction of her hunger after their first few nights together. Strangely, her attraction for him seemed merely to balloon and spread until she swore she could come if he blew on her the right way.

Another moan from the next room followed by words she couldn't make out. Marie's mouth stilled and she stared into Ian's eyes. She pulled back and swallowed hard.

Ian cleared his throat and stroked her breast through her blouse.

"What's say we give them a run for their money?" he murmured, nibbling on her ear.

What?

He wasn't…he couldn't be…was he suggesting that they make enough noise to rival his roommate and his lady, as if this were some sort of contest?

Another low moan and the squeak of springs.

Marie licked her lips, suddenly restless. The mere

suggestion should have repulsed her. But somewhere in the shadows of her psyche she discovered she was more than a little turned on by the idea. She idly wondered what the prize would be for the winning couple....

Her answer to Ian's suggestion was purely of the physical variety, because she was afraid that if she said anything, she'd snap out of the period of temporary insanity, and because she was so hot, she burned. She pushed him back on his bed with a loud squeak of his own bedsprings, then yanked her shirt up over her head.

"Remember, you asked for this."

11

OH, BOY.

Ian had a hard time remembering his own name as he watched Marie hastily strip down to nothing in front of him, the faint light filtering in through the window turning her sweet skin to the color of fresh cream.

She leaned down where he lay across the bed and tugged on the front of his shirt. "You're still dressed."

Ian stared down at himself, surprised that he was. The way he figured it, he should have been naked immediately.

He reached for the buttons to his shirt, but a small, firm breast swayed in front of his eyes, completely distracting him. His hands moved to Marie instead, pinching her pert nipples between his index fingers and thumbs, his gaze glued to the long line of her neck as she stretched her head back and made a soft sound in her throat. He pulled her right nipple deep into his mouth, swirling his tongue around it, immediately lost in the taste and texture of her.

When she looked back down at him, the predatory expression on her face spoke volumes. "Get out of those clothes. Now."

Ian was only too happy to oblige. But alternating between touching her tempting flesh and seeing to his clothes was ultimately too much to concentrate on, and he forgot about his clothes and instead rolled her over onto her back, barely managing to open his fly and sheathe himself with a condom before driving all the way between her hot, hot thighs.

Her combination gasp and moan increased his own desire tenfold. He had no doubt that his noisy roommate had heard her. Hell, the entire building and anyone within a half-mile radius had probably heard her cry out. But Ian couldn't bring himself to care. He slowly slid out, then drove all the way home again, watching as Marie bunched the white top sheet in her fists and gritted her teeth against another groan.

But Ian wasn't about to make it easy on her. He grasped her legs and bent them until they were between them, his chest against her slender shins as he withdrew and rammed deep into her again.

She cried out, her fingers releasing the sheet and grabbing instead for his shoulders where she dug her nails deep into his flesh.

Ian established a relentless rhythm, rendering her completely motionless while he stroked her again and again and again.

"Please," Marie moaned, her breathing coming in rapid gasps, sweat glistening on her throat and breasts. "I...need to move."

Ian fought to hold their position, barely aware of the squeak of the bedsprings, the silence from the other room or Marie's attempt to free her legs. The only thing he heard was the thud of his own heartbeat.

"Not yet..." he heard Marie whimper. "Oh, no, not..."

A long moan stopped the flow of words as her fingernails dug more deeply into his shoulders, shoving him toward his own crisis.

IF MARIE THOUGHT HAVING secretive sex in a seedy motel room was decadent, being with Ian in his bedroom while another couple were going at it in the next room was doubly so.

No sooner was she finishing one climax than she was rushing headlong into another.

She straddled Ian then stared down at where he was nestled between her thighs, sweat trickling down the length of her spine, her breasts seeming to shiver with pure need as she took him inside of her. She'd heard Jena occasionally talk about her own fantasies of group sex. Well, at least until Tommy Brodie had come into her life and her friend had finally settled down—if you could call what Jena was doing settling down. But the mere mention of sex with more than two people had made Marie grimace. But now...

A small voice in the back of her mind told her she should be ashamed of herself. Good Italian-American Catholic girls shouldn't be thinking such wicked thoughts. But another voice told her that she wasn't about to remove the wall between her and Ian and the other couple. And what they were doing was the closest she'd come to group sex. Anyway, she certainly wasn't about to confess this to her parish priest. She'd probably give the old guy a heart attack.

Ian thrust deep inside her, shooting flames through her belly and making her realize that she was neglecting her duties as his lover. She smiled down at him, then pressed her palms against his flat nipples. "My...impatient, aren't we?" She wet one of her fingers then swirled the tip around his right nipple.

He growled. "I'm going to take away your riding privileges if you don't run this horse."

She laughed, then clucked her tongue. "Let a guy

between your legs and look what happens. He turns into a…man.''

Ian skimmed his fingers down her sides while his thumbs trailed a line toward the V of her legs. He pressed both digits against her pulsing core and she gasped. Noisily.

Marie shivered all over. She couldn't remember being so…loud before. She'd always subscribed to the notion that she should keep quiet, keep her feelings to herself. And, for God's sake, never let anyone hear her because Lord only knew what the neighbors would think.

Only this time she knew exactly what the neighbors were thinking…and exactly what they were doing, as well. And the knowledge turned her on more than she would have ever imagined.

''Marie…'' Ian said in a low voice.

She opened her mouth to respond only to have her breath whoosh out instead as he rolled her over, then turned her over, positioning her doggie style.

Holy cow.

He entered her with one long stroke, filling her to overflowing, forcing her to hold on tight or else lose her balance. Her arms shook, and she suspected her knees would have knocked if they could, as her entire body shuddered.

Ian grasped her hips then opened her to him farther with simple pressure on her buttocks. Marie arched her back and thrust her bottom into the air to give him easier access, then moaned when he filled her a second time, his warm sac swaying against her swollen womanhood. She reached between her own legs and gently grasped his balls in her fingers, forcing him to still or else risk serious injury as she pressed the globes against her more intimately.

Wow....

She released him only to feel him surge up into her again and again, his flesh slapping against hers, the chaos building to a feverish pitch as the headboard slammed against the wall separating them from the other couple.

"Not...yet," Ian said, echoing her words from a short time before.

Marie used every ounce of strength to hold off her own climax. She strained against him, grinding mindlessly, insatiably, until her own orgasm hit like a big, wet hurricane. And it swept him right up along with her, if his guttural groan was any indication. And she was pretty convinced it was, because he went completely still, his fingers holding almost painfully onto her flesh. His erection bucked inside her, drawing out her own crisis and coaxing yet another sound of deep satisfaction from her throat.

Ian collapsed against her back and she collapsed to the bed, completely incapable of drawing enough air into her burning lungs.

"I...can't...breathe," she whispered.

Ian instantly rolled off of her.

She smiled. "That's...not...what I meant."

He possessively curled his fingers into her dripping curls and gave a gentle tug. "I know."

A soft tap came from the other side of the wall, nearly startling Marie.

"Bravo, Ian. You win."

Marie stared into Ian's sexy, sweat-coated face, then burst out laughing.

"I THINK WE'VE SCARED them off."

Ian lazily ran his fingertips up and down Marie's

bare back. Their heartbeats had returned to normal. The sweat had dried. And the February temperatures were cool enough for him to pull his comforter up to cover them both to the waist. But only that far. He couldn't bear to cover up Marie's delectable body any farther.

He leaned back and looked down where her head rested against his chest. He half expected to find her sleeping. Instead she was staring at the opposite wall, wide awake. And suspiciously quiet.

Uh-oh.

Nowhere was the languid half smile he usually saw after incredible sex—and this time had been the best yet. Not a trace of satisfaction, contentment or passion was to be seen on her beautiful face.

He began to take his arm from around her. "Are you hungry?"

She snuggled closer, barring his escape. "Nope."

He swallowed thickly. "Oh."

She glanced at him and smiled. But before he could return it, she stopped smiling.

Double uh-oh.

After a few moments, she said quietly, "You know, Frankie Jr. knows about us."

He stared at her, certain he had misheard. Because if Frankie Jr. knew about them, then that meant the entire Bertelli clan did, and depending on when they'd found out they would have been pounding on his door long before now.

She cleared her throat. "I mean, he doesn't know *know*, but he does know I've been meeting someone."

Ian's muscles instantly relaxed. "Then he's not as dumb as I thought he was."

Marie lightly smacked his bare arm. "Knock it off."

He chuckled and laid his hand against her back again. She was so incredibly soft and warm. "I thought you were going to say he knew about us. As in, who I was. I thought maybe he recognized my voice on the phone earlier or something."

He watched her pull her plump bottom lip into her mouth, then sigh. "I think I want to tell him."

"Who? Frankie Jr.?"

She stared at him.

"Tell him what? About us? Me?"

She nodded faintly. "Yeah."

"Why in the hell would you want to go and do a dumb fool thing like that for?"

She lifted her head and began to move away from him. This time he refused *her* escape.

Okay, so maybe saying what he had hadn't been the wisest choice. But the words had just tumbled out of his mouth on the heels of her simple, yet very complicated and problematic, statement.

"Whoa. Was it something I said?" he asked, trying to soothe her with a light caress. Only it wasn't working. Her muscles were as taut and inflexible as his take on this conversation.

She blinked up at him, her lashes casting shadows against her cheeks. "Not so much what you said, but what you didn't say."

Ian shook his head. "I'm not following you here." Problem was, he was afraid he knew exactly where she was heading. And he wasn't anywhere near ready for the journey. He'd just returned from Chicago. Landed a position at one of the most prestigious law firms in Albuquerque. Was this close to a full partnership with

Frankie's case. The last thing on his mind was a committed relationship. Not just with Marie, with anyone.

But somehow he didn't think telling her that would help matters any. His experience with women was that it never did.

He felt her gaze on him for a long time before she said, "Tell me, Ian, have you ever thought about where this is going?"

Ian's brows rushed up on his forehead. Bam. There it was. The question all men dreaded. But him especially. Because not only was his confirmed bachelor status hanging in the balance, but his physical well-being right alongside it.

Marie gestured with her hand. "I mean...this."

She wriggled for him to let go again and this time he did. More out of fear and distraction than anything else.

She lay back against the pillows and stared at the ceiling, then quietly cleared her throat. "When the motel burned down today...when I talked to you on the phone earlier...I don't know..."

Ian forced himself to look relaxed but his heart was going a million miles a minute.

She turned her head toward him. "I thought I might not see you again."

Yikes. The end of fantastic sex played out through his mind like the closing credits of a movie. "Our paths would have crossed at the courthouse."

"That's not what I meant."

"I know."

The funny thing was, she knew that he knew.

Marie lay back against the pillows again, as puzzled as Ian apparently was by her line of questioning.

Line of questioning? She wasn't in a courtroom. She

was in a bedroom. With a man she'd just had incredible, mind-blowing sex with. Yet somehow she felt she'd be more comfortable in a courtroom right at that moment.

She inhaled a deep breath, then held it. What was she thinking? She'd gone into this…affair with the same expectations Ian had. She'd been after the sex, pure and simple.

So why the change now? Why did she suddenly want more?

She supposed it could be a number of factors. The destruction of their usual meeting place. Her confusing conversation with Frankie Jr. earlier that night. Or the fact that despite her strange excitement over having sex at the same time as Ian's roommate in the next room, she didn't like that she was in a bedroom she'd never seen inside an apartment she wouldn't be able to describe if someone held a gun to her head.

A burst of pride exploded through. So, she wanted more. What was the crime in that? What was wrong with wanting to move her relationship with Ian from a private to a public level? She wanted to go out to dinner with him and not worry that the owner was calling her father before their pasta was brought to the table. She wanted to tell her family that…that…

That what?

Her throat grew tight.

She wanted to tell them that for the first time in her life she was in love.

Oh, boy.

She stared at the ceiling as if half expecting it to fall on her.

Yes, she realized with a jolting start. She did love Ian. In all likelihood she probably had always loved

Ian, from the first time she laid eyes on him when she was thirteen. Sure, back then it had been puppy love. But surely when he had stolen her virginity right out from under her nose at the age of eighteen she'd been adult enough to know her own heart.

Of course, she would never have admitted it then.

She was surprised she was even admitting to it now.

But what was it they said about bags and cats? Once out the damn things were impossible to get back in?

If only she didn't feel like a wild tom was ripping her insides out right that minute, maybe she could concentrate on the conversation she was trying to have. Trying, but apparently failing miserably.

The sheets rustled as Ian started to get up. "I'm going to go get something to eat."

"Wait." Marie bolted upright and grabbed his hand, even further surprising herself. "Wait," she whispered again.

The dim light from the window caught him full in the face, showing his confusion, and his growing emotional distance from her.

Well, this was going to be easy, wasn't it? she thought sarcastically.

She didn't say anything for a long time. She couldn't be sure how long, but she did know that she'd swallowed thickly no fewer than a half a dozen times.

"What is it, Marie?" Ian asked quietly.

She slowly removed her hand, then curled her knees to her chest and covered them with the comforter. "I don't know. I just want this…you and me…to be normal."

She watched him grin. "Ah, but you forget. What we share isn't anywhere near normal. It's paranormal."

That almost brought a smile to her face. Almost.

"I want to tell my family."

She could have sworn he made a choking sound, although his expression didn't reveal so much as a flinch.

"Ian?"

"Hmm?"

"I said I want to tell my family. About you. Us."

He remained silent for several long, heart-stopping moments. Then he finally said, "Are you insane?"

He got up from the bed, paced one way, then the other. Marie wasn't sure how she felt about having her common sense questioned, but she was willing to give him the benefit of the doubt simply because he was so worked up.

"Marie, I...don't you think...I mean..." Suddenly he stopped and stared at her, his face in shadow. "You tell your father, and I'm as good as dead," he said in a no-nonsense, point-blank manner.

She frowned at him, part of her wondering how much of his comment had to do with how much he bought into the mafia stigma. Another part of her pondered whether or not this was some sort of lame excuse designed to keep their relationship exactly the way it was.

She crossed her arms and said quietly but evenly, "If I don't tell them, then this relationship is as good as dead."

He didn't answer her.

Then again, maybe his silence was his answer.

"I'm going to get something to eat. You want something?"

Marie didn't answer. Not that she could have. Her throat had closed up on her as she watched him walk bare-assed right from the room.

WHY COULDN'T WOMEN JUST leave well enough alone? Why did they always have to ruin everything? Control it? Move the pieces of their lives around like they were so many blocks they were trying to place just so?

Ian resecured the towel around his waist. He'd grabbed it from the bathroom on his way to the kitchen when he realized he'd virtually run from his bedroom in his birthday suit. Now he stood staring at the pathetic contents of his refrigerator. He closed that door and opened the freezer. Frozen, individual servings of Stroganoff and lamb stew that his mother had sent home with him last week stared back at him, along with all the store-bought stuff.

Okay, so maybe Marie Bertelli wasn't just any woman to him. In all honesty, she had never been just another conquest, another notch on his headboard. There had always been something about her…

Oh, no. He was not going to go down that road.

He pulled a frozen pizza out of the freezer, slammed the door, then jerkily tore at the packaging. He paused long enough to scan the instructions, then inserted his thumb where the package told him to. It opened easily. No doubt a woman had probably designed the damn thing.

Now, if he could find the directions to one certain Marie Bertelli, he'd be all set.

He opened the microwave, threw the pizza inside, then entered the time.

Ian stared at the revolving carousel through the tinted window. How many times had he stood exactly where he was standing now? Not physically, but figuratively? A dozen? Possibly more? The time frame always differed. Some women he'd dated had wanted to go serious one day into the relationship. Others it had taken a couple of months. But eventually they all led to exactly the crossroads he faced now.

Only this time one of the roads had a family of Bertellis standing in his path.

Good God, what had he been thinking?

It didn't escape his notice that this time loomed different, somehow, though. He'd never seriously even considered the other road, but chosen the path that left the relationship behind, that allowed him to hold on to his bachelor status.

Now...

The microwave dinged and he jumped.

Now he had completely, utterly, totally lost his marbles.

He grabbed a kitchen towel and carefully took the hot pizza from the microwave. He caught movement from the corner of his eye just as the heat seeped through the towel and burned his hands.

He turned to put the food on the counter. "Do you want—"

His words lodged solidly in his throat. Marie hadn't simply changed her mind about being hungry, put on one of his shirts and come to join him. She was fully dressed, her coat on, and was heading for the door.

Jesus...

"Ah!" It took a second for the heat blasting his hands to sink through his state of shock. He dropped the pizza, missing the counter by a good inch so that the pizza fell top down right on top of his foot.

Marie stared at him, the pizza, then turned and walked through his front door.

MARIE COLLAPSED AGAINST Ian's condo door and swallowed hard. In that one moment, she came to understand what Mona had been talking about when she'd said that Barry would rather risk breaking his neck falling from her window than make their relationship public.

She'd seen those same elements on Ian's face a few moments before.

She rubbed her forehead and pushed from the wood. He didn't want to go public with their relationship. He wanted to keep things between them exactly as they were. No complications. No progress. Nothing but great sex.

She knew a moment of pause. There *was* the great sex...

She pushed from the door and hurried down the steps. No. She wouldn't do it. No matter how great the sex, she was not going to stay in a relationship with no future beyond the bedroom.

Relationship? She stepped out into the cold night air, wondering if that was even how you could classify what had happened between her and Ian. No. They didn't have a relationship. They'd had a convenient...arrangement. A series of midnight trysts designed to see to some primal human needs. Nothing more, nothing less. At least not for him. Just seeing the look on his face when she was leaving told her everything and more than she needed to know. Yes, part of the grimace on his face might have been caused by hot cheese, but the rest...the rest told her he didn't want anything from her outside of the bedroom.

She opened the door to her Mustang then slid behind the wheel, the fact that she'd used the past tense in reference to Ian and her very sobering, indeed.

And that's what had to happen now, wasn't it? She couldn't possibly go back up to his apartment or back to the way things were. No matter how much she might have wanted to, there was no stuffing that big, wild, scary cat back into the bag it had jumped out of.

"Marie!"

Her eyes widened as she watched Ian bolt from the front door of his apartment building wearing nothing but a fluffy white towel. He was running toward her car, waving one arm.

Marie turned the ignition and put the car in gear, her heart hammering against her chest. She was afraid that if she let him get to the car, she would end up going back. And she couldn't do that.

She pressed the clutch and gas and sped from the parking space just as Ian's hold on his towel slipped.

As she turned onto the street, she watched in her rearview mirror as Ian stopped in the middle of the asphalt wearing nothing but a heart-jerking frown, the night breeze catching his towel and hurtling it for the pines edging the lot.

If anything deserved a laugh, that sight did.

Why then did Marie only feel like crying?

12

As far as plans went, Marie expected this one to work about as well as the others she had made lately. Which was absolutely not at all.

She sat in the corner booth at Little Italia and resisted the desire to fold her arms on the wood table, then plop her head down on top of them. She'd been to the Italian restaurant on countless occasions throughout her life. But the only meal she could concentrate on was the one she'd shared with Ian.

Four days. Four long, grueling days of silence from Ian, relentless questions from Frankie Jr. and tedious progress on all of her cases. All and all, her life loomed a complete and utter mess.

And as she watched her sister-in-law Toni walk toward the table, she had the distinct impression that things were going to get much, much worse before they got better.

"Oh, thank God you gave me the perfect excuse to get out of the house today," Toni said, kissing both of Marie's cheeks, then shrugging out of her coat and sitting down. "Lunch is something I desperately need. A nice, long, three-hour lunch filled with nothing but girl talk. Adult girl talk."

Marie smiled. She'd always genuinely liked Frankie Jr.'s wife. While Antoinette Guiliano had been a few grades ahead of her throughout school, she'd always been darkly beautiful and had a reputation for being straight shooting and honest. Almost painfully so.

Then she'd married Frankie and become a great wife and mother to boot. Marie would hate her on the spot if she didn't already love her.

"Frankie the third and Anthony a little much today?"

Toni rolled her eyes and nearly sucked down the entire contents of the glass of Chianti the waiter poured for her. When she finished, she animatedly nodded her head. "You can say that again." She raised a hand. "But I'm not going to talk about them today. I came here to talk about you."

Marie blinked at her. "Me?"

Toni folded her hands on top of the table, gave a furtive look around to make sure no one was listening, then leaned forward. "Frankie tells me you're having man trouble."

Marie was sure she'd just been launched into a parallel universe.

Surely she wasn't sitting there listening to her sister-in-law asking about her sex life when her own husband was camping out on Marie's couch and had been for the past week?

"Frankie told you that?"

Toni nodded and placed her napkin across her lap. "Uh-huh. The other day. Says you're a pain to live with lately."

"Yes, well, I wouldn't be living with him if you hadn't kicked him out," Marie blurted.

Toni stared at her as if she'd just been slapped.

Marie collapsed against the booth and groaned. "Oh, Toni, I'm sorry. I don't know what's gotten into me lately. I seem to be snapping at everyone. And I haven't even been over to see Ma for a week.''

''So she told me.''

''You talked to Ma?''

Toni grabbed a breadstick. ''Of course I talked to Ma. I talk to her every day.''

''But...''

''But what?''

''But how do you keep hidden the fact that Frankie and you are...having problems?''

''That's easy.'' She shrugged as she crunched into he breadstick. ''Frankie never talks to her on the phone. And I...well, I just talk about the kids nonstop.'' She swept crumbs from the table in front of her. ''The only trouble I run into is when she asks when we're stopping by. I mean I took the kids over the other day, but she keeps pressing for all of us to come for dinner.''

''What do you say?''

''So far I've come up with some good excuses. You know, my sister's baby shower, my mother needs help spring cleaning. But I'm running dry pretty quick here.'' She sighed. ''Have you ordered yet?''

''Appetizers,'' Marie said, avoiding her sister-in-law's gaze. ''Enough for both of us. I thought, you know, that we could talk a bit before we ordered our entrées.''

Toni looked at her for a long moment, then smiled. ''Sounds good.''

As if on cue, the waiter brought nearly every appetizer on the menu because Marie hadn't been able to make up her mind. She'd been completely incapable of thinking clearly enough to remember what Toni liked or disliked. She covertly glanced at her watch. Besides, she had twenty-five more minutes to warm her sister-in-law up to the idea of a third guest joining them.

Marie had to concentrate so as not to choke on her own wine. She only hoped that this lunch went better than the one with Mona had. But the way her luck was running…well, she was half afraid local law enforcement might be required to break up the resulting fight.

"Anyway, enough about me," Toni said, filling her plate with a little bit of everything. "I want to hear about you."

Marie made a face as she forced herself to fill her own plate. She'd been ceaselessly ravenous only a few days ago, whereas now she had zero appetite. In fact, Frankie Jr. had had to cook the last couple of nights. And as much as she hated to admit it, he'd done a pretty good job.

Yeah, well, if he did it more at home maybe he still wouldn't be camped out on her sofa.

She absently chewed some garlic bread, tasting nothing of it. Something bothered her about this entire conversation—Toni's casual attitude about her and Frankie Jr.'s separation, for one thing. A thought bounced around inside her mind, but she couldn't quite latch onto it.

Marie shrugged. "There's not much to tell, really. I was seeing someone and now I'm not." She shrugged again. "No big deal."

Only it was a big deal, wasn't it? She couldn't sleep, couldn't eat, and if she didn't straighten up pretty soon she'd go home to her apartment to find her mother had had all her things moved back home.

"Doesn't look that way to me," Toni said. "Who is he?"

Marie stared at her sister-in-law. "Did Frankie Jr. put you up to this?"

"Frankie didn't put me up to anything." Toni pointed at her. "You're the one who invited me to lunch. Remember?"

"Oh, yes. Right."

Toni narrowed her eyes. "Why did you invite me to lunch anyway?"

"What?"

Toni wiped her hands together and focused her full attention on Marie. Marie fought not to fidget.

"Well, it doesn't look like you're much up for girl talk," Toni said. "When Frankie told me that you had been seeing someone, I thought maybe you might like a shoulder to cry on."

Marie gave an inelegant snort, then hid behind her napkin. "Um, no. That's the last thing on my agenda."

And the first thing on her agenda would be walking through that door in a manner of minutes.

"Anyway, if I wanted a shoulder to cry on, it wouldn't be because of someone I was seeing," Marie continued. "It would be because my brother is driving me absolutely, one-hundred-percent insane."

Toni smiled. "Yeah, he's good at that, isn't he?"

Marie leaned forward. "So tell me, when, exactly, do I get my life and my apartment back?"

A cloud skidded through Toni's eyes before she turned them back to focus on her plate.

That was it. The thought that had been bouncing around Marie's head finally plopped right down in the middle of it, clear as day.

Her brother and his wife's problem really wasn't all that different from what she and Ian, and Mona and Barry were going through. Well, okay, there were some important differences. Namely that Toni and Frankie were married. But beyond that, there were some very striking similarities.

The biggest of which was that it was happening in secret.

Her parents didn't know that Frankie had moved into her place. At work, if the guys needed anything, they called Toni who then called Frankie at Marie's. And Marie was pretty sure that Toni had probably concocted some cockamamie story to explain Frankie's absence from the house to friends and neighbors.

So if nobody knew about it, then it wasn't real, was it? And if it wasn't real, you didn't have to deal with it.

Oh, boy.

Marie looked up to find the prime reason for Toni and Frankie's problems walking through the front door.

"Who's that?" Toni asked, apparently catching Marie's interest.

"Someone I invited to have lunch with us." Marie stood up to welcome the new addition. "Toni Bertelli, I think it's long past time you met Lola."

Damn, but she looked good.

Damn, he wished he'd never agreed to allow her to cocounsel her father's case.

Ian rubbed the back of his neck. Had it really been four days since he'd last seen Marie? It felt like a lifetime ago. As he sat in the firm's conference room with her and Frankie Sr. he kept thinking he noticed changes in her. Had her hair grown longer? Had she lost weight? Then he'd remind himself that only four days had passed since she'd literally left him flapping in the wind as she squealed out of the parking lot. He told himself he really shouldn't care if she wasn't eating right. But the truth was that he did.

Experience told him that all women eventually reached a stage where they wanted more. What surprised him was that he hadn't seen it coming from Marie. He'd assumed that, like him, she'd been in it strictly for the sex. And now that he saw how very wrong he'd been, he wasn't sure what his next step should be. Or if there should even be a next step. All he knew was that he missed her like hell.

"So you think they're about to issue an arrest warrant for my father," Marie summed up what he'd been saying for the past ten minutes, bringing Marie and Frankie Sr. up to speed on what had been going on between him and the U.S. Treasury agents.

"Yes," he said simply.

Frankie Bertelli Sr. sat back and dry-washed his face with his hands. "I can't believe it. All my life I strive to make an honest living. And now when I'm a few years from retirement, I'm facing prison time for something I didn't do."

Ian looked at the older man. He'd never outright asked Frankie Sr. whether he'd done what he was accused of. Had never had the guts. But now that the man had offered up the information voluntarily, Ian found that he believed him. Unequivocally.

Marie squeezed her father's hand and looked at Ian. Her pained expression was like a sucker punch to the gut. "Has there been any progress at all on locating Uncle Nunzio?"

"The Treasury Department isn't looking beyond what they've already found. Namely, the blood from Nunzio's car. Well, that and they're dragging the, um, Rio Grande river." He tried to ignore Marie's wince.

He shrugged and closed his case folder. "Our private detectives haven't been able to turn up squat, either. It's as if he just up and disappeared from the face of the Earth."

"But your detectives are still looking?" she asked.

Ian nodded. "They're still looking."

Frankie Sr. glanced at his daughter. "What am I going to tell your mama? If I get arrested, it'll kill her."

Ian could tell that Marie was more concerned about what was going to happen to her father as she patted his hand. "Ma will be fine. Let's just concentrate on how we're going to get you out of this mess."

"WHAT IN THE HELL WERE you thinking?" Frankie Jr. asked Marie the instant she came through her apartment door. "You took Lola and Toni to lunch? Together? Are you stupid, or what?"

Marie stood completely still as the door behind her closed. Her feet were killing her. She was wearing her work clothes and was still clutching her briefcase. She hadn't even taken a breath in her own place yet and her brother was laying into her.

Not exactly a banner day.

Frankie Jr. paced the length of her apartment then back again. He stared at her, then shook his head and began pacing again.

Marie put her briefcase down next to the door, stepped out of her shoes, then sighed.

"Okay, so maybe it wasn't the brightest idea I ever had," she grudgingly admitted, remembering what had transpired earlier at Little Italia restaurant.

It hadn't been pretty. While Toni had never met Lola and didn't know her on sight, she was more than familiar with the other woman's name. And the instant

Marie said it in introduction, Toni had taken the con-
ciliatory hand Lola had offered and used it to pull the
other woman facedown onto all the appetizers the table
boasted. Even before Marie could explain, or the wait-
ers could help Lola, Toni had grabbed her purse and
coat, stared at Marie as if Toni were an inch away from
shoving her face into the food as well, then stormed
from the restaurant on a black cloud.

Marie absently rubbed her forehead. A little over an
hour after that fiasco, she'd learned not only that her
father was on the verge of being arrested, but that her
attraction to Ian was still so strong that not even the
doom of the situation had been enough to stop her from
spinning fantasies of having Ian right there on his glass
desk.

"Brightest?" Frankie echoed as he stopped in front
of her and pointed a finger at her temple. "Hands
down, this is the stupidest thing you've ever done. Do
you know Lola's talking lawsuit? Hell, Uncle Manny
had to talk her out of calling the cops right there on
the spot."

Marie batted his hand away, very quickly losing the
loose hold she had on her own Italian temper. "Well,
that would have made two Bertellis slated for the slammer then, wouldn't it?" she muttered under her breath.
She briefly entertained the idea of making it a full three
by doing away with her brother right there and then.

Frankie Jr. glared at her.

She glared back. "What? Hell, I don't blame Lola
for wanting to call the police. What Toni did was rude
and...outrageous."

"Well, how in the hell did you expect her to react?
For God's sake, Marie, she thinks I'm banging the
woman and here you go and invite her to lunch. What

did you think would happen? You'd introduce them and over some rigatoni the two of them would become best friends?''

Marie sputtered for a few moments, then her spine snapped upright. ''Well…yes, I did.''

Frankie snorted then began pacing again. Marie found herself pacing right after him. ''What? Is it too much to ask for some reason to enter the equation here? Then excuse the hell out of me for thinking that everyone involved would at least act civilized, for fuck's sake.''

He stopped and blinked slightly at her. It dawned on Marie that it was because of her use of the ''f'' word.

''What? You didn't know I swore? Fuck, fuck, fuck. How do you like that, big brother?''

He started to crack a grin.

Absolutely the wrong thing to do at that moment.

Marie had had just about enough of being the dutiful daughter, the sympathetic sister, the secretive lover. All were passive roles and she was itching to take some very real action.

She pointed her finger at Frankie Jr. ''Don't you dare laugh.''

He rubbed his chin and his grin widened.

''Okay, that's it.''

She stalked into her bedroom, grabbed an empty laundry basket, then began piling his things—the number of which had accumulated over the past week—inside. A trip to the bathroom and a sweep of her hand on the back of the commode and she was done. She opened her apartment door and deposited the basket in the hall, leaving the door wide open.

She turned to find Frankie Jr. standing in the same spot she'd left him.

"Out," she said simply.

He blinked at her several times, the damnable grin finally disappearing from his disgustingly handsome face. "What?"

"You heard me. I want you out. Now."

"Aw, come on, Marie. One little fight and you're booting me?"

She spotted a small pile of sports magazines on her coffee table and swiftly added them to the basket in the hall. Give the guy an inch, and he takes a mile. In one week he'd managed to turn her apartment into his. And she was sick of it. She'd had it up to here.

"Where will I go?"

She stared at him. "I...don't...care. Just so long as it's not here." She held out her hand palm up. "Key."

"What?"

"My key."

He slowly pulled out his ring from his jeans pocket and made a production out of looking for the right one.

He sighed and let his hands flop back to his sides. "Toni won't let me back in now. You know that, don't you? She thinks I put you up to the whole thing with Lola."

"I...don't...care," Marie repeated. "Stay in a hotel. Go terrorize our brothers and their wives. Sleep in your car, for pete's sake. Go cry on Ma's shoulder. I... don't...care."

Frankie Jr.'s face went white at the mention of their mother.

He did not make a move.

Marie paced toward the kitchen where she snatched the cordless off its perch. She held it up and waved it at him. "I'll give you to the count of three. If you're not outside my door by then, I call Ma and tell her everything.''

"You wouldn't."

"Wanna try me?" Marie asked steadily, giving him a saucy smile.

Her brother didn't look like he was ready to take the risk. In fact, he looked downright terrified that she would follow through on her threat.

"Okay. Okay. I'm going."

Marie held the phone until she saw him step out into the hall. She closed the door after him, then opened it again.

"My key." She held out her hand, ignoring his hopeful look. Apparently he had thought she had changed her mind when she opened the door.

He sighed and took the copy of the key off his keychain and handed it to her.

Marie palmed it, then closed the door again.

For long minutes she stood on the other side, leaning against the cool wood, waiting for guilt to assault her. Strangely, all she felt was relief.

She glanced down at the phone she still held. She didn't know whether she had it in her to actually follow through on the threat to call her mother. Thankfully, she hadn't had to find out.

The extension rang, nearly chasing her from her skin. Caller ID was on the base so she didn't know who it might be. Ian, maybe?

"Hello?"

Her mother's voice came over the line. "This is how you treat your mother? For one week my oldest boy is staying with you and you don't tell me?"

Marie slid down the door to sit on the floor, wondering if it were at all possible for things to get any worse.

TWELVE O'CLOCK AND ALL was not well.

Ian stretched across his bed, mentally grabbing for one single, solitary thing to be thankful for in that one moment. He pulled his head back and stared at his pillow. He could be thankful for his pillow. The only problem was it smelled like Marie, and his body's instantaneous physical response was not pretty.

"You can be thankful you even have a bed," he muttered, rolling over so that his nose wasn't in the middle of his pillow and surrounded by Marie's subtle, provocative scent.

Yes, indeed, he could be thankful that there was anything left in the apartment at all. He'd returned home to find the place completely cleaned out. He'd immediately thought there'd been a break-in. Instead, he'd found a note from his roommate Tyler and discovered there had been a breakout instead. And Tyler had taken everything that wasn't nailed down with him.

Except for the contents of Ian's bedroom.

Well, okay, he suspected a few of his suits and sweaters were missing, and there was his brand new black leather jacket, but he wasn't up to inventorying what was missing from his wardrobe. All his brand new furniture, sound equipment, home theatre and the entire contents of his kitchen including the frozen dinners loomed more important just then.

"Thanks for the memories, dude," the note had read. "Take care." Signed, "Ty."

He should have booted the SOB out long before now. As it stood, he'd spent the past three hours talking to the reporting officers, with very little hope for recovery of his property. Unless he'd had his things engraved, good luck trying to prove what was his and what was his roommate's since they'd shared the place for the past three months. It meant very little that everything had been Ian's, that the only thing Tyler had brought was a waterbed—which was against condo rules—and little more than the clothes on his back.

Then, on top of all that, all he could think about was how damn good Marie had looked earlier that afternoon and how damn much he itched to be with her right now. Crush his mouth to hers. Mold her body to his. Make her pant and sweat and cry out with need...

He scrubbed his face with his hands and sighed heavily. This was far worse than he ever imagined it would be. Hell, it wasn't the first time a woman had figured out that his settling down wasn't in the cards. He had a career to build. Everything else came a very distant second. And if they couldn't understand that, well, they knew where the door was.

The problem was Marie knew where the door was without him even pointing it out. He hadn't even had to say anything. No speech on why they should remain as they were. No careful explanations about how the future was a vast wilderness to him to be explored...alone. She'd gotten the picture without his having to paint it for her. And she'd walked.

Maybe that was it. The reason the whole situation bothered him so much. Because, in this case, he hadn't been the dumper, but rather the dumpee. And it didn't agree with him. Not at all.

No. Even as he thought about it, and managed to work up a little remorse, he knew that wasn't why he was lying there staring at the ceiling and wondering what she was doing right that minute. Something more was at the root of his…strange state. And he was not ready to go there. *So* not ready. And he didn't think he ever would be.

Still, that didn't stop him from wishing Marie were lying next to him right now. On his terms. Which meant no talk of any future beyond the next few minutes and a superb orgasm.

But that wasn't going to happen when her father was a pair of handcuffs away from being arrested for a crime he didn't commit. And not when he knew that once Marie had something stuck in her head, there it would remain forever and a day.

Ian lay still for long, quiet minutes, trying to calm his breathing and steady his heartbeat. But his brain and body were having none of it. Ten minutes later he got up, still fully clothed, and walked through his gapingly empty apartment, grabbed his coat and listened as the sound of the closing door echoed inside.

13

MARIE SLOWLY AWAKENED TO find her face smashed against the sofa cushion, a cheese puff attached to her forehead and Conan O'Brien on the TV across the room pulling a face that could have been meant directly for her. Somewhere in the back of her mind she registered that the telephone was ringing and had in all likelihood awakened her. Or else she'd be staring at Matt Lauer right now instead of Conan O'Brien.

She pushed herself to a sitting position, then searched for the cordless where it must have fallen down into the sofa cushions. Great, just great. The first night in how many that she could sleep in her own bed and she'd fallen asleep on the couch.

She finally found the phone and pushed the button to answer it. "Hello, hello?" she said before she had the receiver to her ear.

"Marie?"

Ian!

She instantly leapt from the couch and tried to straighten herself as if he was at the door rather than on the phone. Only after she slammed her knee against the coffee table did it dawn on her why he would be calling her at—she glanced at her watch—one o'clock in the morning.

Oh, God…

"It's Dad, isn't it? They've arrested him," she whispered, collapsing back to the sofa.

"You're right, this is about your father…"

Marie idly pulled the bag of cheese curls she'd sat on out from under her, then reached for the remote. Within seconds Conan's quirky face disappeared, plunging her apartment, not unlike her life, into complete darkness.

"How fast can you get to the hospital?"

Marie's heart squeezed so tightly she was afraid she might be in need of a hospital herself pretty quick. "Why? What's wrong?"

"No, no, nothing's wrong," he said quickly. "Just get down here. And meet me in intensive care."

He hung up.

Marie stared at the cordless, trying to make sense out of his words. He tells her to get to the hospital, that there's nothing wrong but to meet him in ICU, then hangs up in her ear.

Marie began dialing her parents' house, then disconnected two numbers short.

This was not looking good.

But she wasn't exactly accomplishing anything while attached to her sofa, either.

It took her five minutes flat to splash some cold water on her face, find a pair of sweats, get a comb stuck in her sorry excuse for hair and rush out the door with a coat and…she went back in to get her purse.

Fifteen minutes after that she was inching down the hall of the intensive care unit. The hospital was eerily quiet this late, nothing but the sound of electronic beeps and soft air compressions and the smell of antiseptic and alcohol letting her know there was any life at all.

She grimaced, not liking the direction of her thoughts.

Down at the end of the hall a security guard stood facing away from her. He took a sip of coffee, then headed in the opposite direction before disappearing around the corner. Marie glanced around. There wasn't anyone at the nurses' station. And there was no sign of Ian.

She absently rubbed her arms. She hated hospitals. She guessed that pretty much ninety percent of the population hated hospitals, save for the hypochondriacs who appeared to want to live in them. She peeked into a doorless room. Somehow she got the impression that the patients on this floor fell into the aforementioned ninety percent. Inside lay someone completely wrapped in gauze with tubes going into his nostrils and others seeming to come out of his mouth. She shuddered, reminded of a movie she'd seen recently about an evil-doing mummy. Then again, all mummies seemed to be evildoing. They snuck up on you from behind and—

Someone touched her shoulder and she screamed. And she screamed again when the mummy seemed startled as well, nearly coming up off the bed.

"Shh," Ian said, pulling her from the doorway.

Marie stared at him, not knowing if she should hug him or whack him with the nearest chart.

He frowned. "What happened to your face?"

Marie's hand went to her right cheek. She felt a long crease there, and an indentation on her forehead. Oh, geez. "Sofa burn." She grabbed his arm and led him toward the nurses' station. "What's going on, Ian? Is Dad here? Has something—"

His grin made her toes curl in her tennis shoes. "No, your dad's not here. But someone you know is."

Marie scanned his face, wondering why he was so happy that someone she knew was in the hospital's intensive care unit.

"Come on," he said, leading her down the hall.

Marie began to ask him where he was taking her, but instead bit solidly on her bottom lip for fear that her voice would come out sounding all raspy and pathetic—the way it always sounded when he touched her. It didn't matter that it was her elbow, and that his touch couldn't have been more casual. Electricity arced whenever he got within an inch of her, putting her at his complete mercy. Which was exactly where she didn't want to be right that moment. Or any other moment, come to think of it.

He finally slowed near a door, then motioned for her to enter.

Remembering the mummy a few doors up, Marie shook her head and swallowed, able to think again now that he wasn't touching her. "You first."

He shrugged, then led the way.

Why didn't somebody turn on a light around here? And where in the hell were all the nurses? This was the ICU, right? Shouldn't there be both nurses and doctors milling about the place ready to deal with any crisis? You know, like if Marie should go into cardiac arrest if another mummy jumped out at her?

Okay, he hadn't jumped out at her exactly. But he had been startled. And a mummy startled was not a pretty sight.

Ian moved to the side of an oxygen tent. Marie hesitantly followed after him, resisting the almost overpowering urge to grab on to his arm—for support and so there was no chance they would be separated. But touching Ian probably wasn't a good idea under any circumstances.

"Voilà," Ian said, sweeping out his arm.

Marie squinted at him, then the blurry person on the other side of the clear plastic. Voilà, what? She moved her head closer so that her nose was almost pressed against the plastic. A light switched on overhead. Marie jumped for the second time in as many minutes.

"Sorry," a nurse said, coming in from the connecting rest room. She held a small tray with ice and water. "I should have turned the light on before. At night we like to keep it quiet around here. Allow the patients to maintain their bearings."

And scare the crap out of any unsuspecting visitors, Marie silently added.

The hair on the back of her neck stood up on end. Not because she was still scared or apprehensive. Rather, she wasn't altogether sure she liked the way the young nurse was smiling at Ian.

She looked to find him smiling back at her.

She glared. First at Ian, then at the young woman who could have been a double for Nicole Kidman. A very attractive, very flirtatious Nicole Kidman.

"I'll, um, leave you two alone with Mr. Doe," Nicole said as she put the tray down on the bedside table. "Just buzz me if you need anything."

Marie wanted to buzz her. With a Weedwacker.

The nurse left the room.

"What?" Ian asked, blinking under the scrutiny of her stare.

Marie rolled her eyes. "Oh, just forget it. Pig."

"Pig? Are you calling me a pig?" he asked, his eyes narrowing. "I spend my night chasing down leads when I much rather would have been chasing you around my very empty apartment, then I find Nunzio, and you're calling me a pig?''

''What do you mean empty? Your apartment is very full. Too full. So full that you couldn't turn the lights on for fear that someone might actually see me. You...''

Had he said he'd found Nunzio?

Marie's heart skipped a beat as she stared back at the oxygen tent. With the light on, she could now make out the person on the other side.

''Uncle Nunzio!'' She glanced at Ian. ''Oh my God, it's Uncle Nunzio.''

Ian grinned. ''I know. I found him, remember?''

Marie made a face as she looked for a way around the tent, didn't find one, then instead took her uncle Nunzio's warm, dry hand and gave it a squeeze. ''He's alive.''

''Uh-huh. Very much so.''

''So that means Dad didn't kill him.''

Marie caught her words and stilled.

Had there been a small part of her that feared her father might have had Uncle Nunzio fitted for a pair of cement boots?

No. Absolutely not. Impossible.

Then why had she been so surprised to find him alive?

Ian crossed his arms over his chest. ''Don't worry. My reaction was pretty much the same.''

''Yeah, but you're not Dad's daughter.'' She thunked her forehead with the palm of her hand. ''Why hadn't I thought to look here?''

''Don't stress about it, Marie. Not even our firm's detectives did. They checked against names, but didn't think to check out the possible identities of any John Doe's.''

''What happened? I mean, how did he end up here?''

EVEN WITH SILLY CREASES in her face, Marie was still so beautiful it almost hurt to look at her. Ian absently rubbed the back of his neck. She wasn't beautiful in the classic sense. Her mouth was a little too wide, but he preferred to see it as generous. Her nose was a little lopsided, but to him it only added to her uniqueness. Her ears, when she tucked all that unruly red hair behind them, protruded in a way that was almost laughable but instead made him want to trace the edges of them.

Okay, sure, he wanted her. Probably even loved her in some deluded, lust-induced sort of way. But what would happen when her family found out that he'd... done her? Then assuming that he survived the week, what would happen after that? A month from now? A year? Would he still think she looked beautiful, get that funny little feeling in the pit of his stomach? Or would he have grown tired of her, think of her as Dumbo rather than beautiful?

And how would she look at him?

It wasn't exactly like he was the catch of a lifetime. He burned ten kinds of red whenever he stepped into the sun. And seeing as they lived in a state that got sun ninety days out of a hundred...well, he'd personally invested in a sunscreen company nearly a decade ago and avoided going outside as much as possible. His diet was for crap. And he obviously didn't have very good taste when it came to choosing roommates.

Of course, he could never imagine Marie taking anything from his place. No. Rather she would probably leave stuff behind. Stuff that would make him crazy when she left him.

What was he talking about? She had already left him. They hadn't been living together, but…

Oh, hell, he was losing it. Lack of sleep and seventy-two hours of sheer hell tended to do that to a guy.

Love and fear of what comes next tended to do that to a guy, too….

"Ian?"

He blinked at Marie. "Huh?"

"I asked how Uncle Nunzio ended up here."

He wished she'd stop calling all her father's friends uncle. It gave him the creeps and made his bones itch for fear that they might end up cracked, or worse, broken.

"Remember his car showed up at the dump? The towing company was supposed to impound it instead. So a simple mistake by an overworked tow-truck driver who just came off a three-day drinking binge came off looking like an attempt to hide evidence."

"But the real evidence wasn't the result of Uncle Nunzio being removed from his car by a strongman, it was the result of a car accident."

"Right."

Marie gasped, remembering the morning her uncle had come up missing. She'd been talking to her mother on her cell phone and had been extra cranky because a car accident had backed up traffic on I-40 for miles.

Uncle Nunzio?

"Anyway," Ian continued, "he's been here for the past two weeks, sans ID, in a coma."

Marie's face went white. "God," she whispered. "I was so happy to see him I didn't think to ask how he's doing."

Ian felt an ache at the look on her face. "His prognosis is still a little sketchy. Massive head and chest injuries. But the nurse says that with each day that passes, his chance for survival increases."

Marie collapsed into a chair next to the bed, her hand still on Nunzio's motionless one. "This is going to kill Dad."

Ian wasn't sure he liked all these references to death. "Have you told him?"

"Who? Frankie Sr.? No. I wanted your confirmation first. I mean, I was pretty sure it was him from his photos, but it was hard to tell." He squinted at her. "You're absolutely sure it's him?"

She nodded. "Positive. See the birthmark on the back of his hand here? He always bragged...brags that it's an outline of Sicily. That he was born with a stamp of his homeland right there on his hand."

Ian thought it could have been Sicily.

Then again, it could have been a gravy stain, too.

"You, um, want to call your dad?"

Marie seemed preoccupied as she stared at the man in the bed. "Hmm?"

Ian turned away from her because he couldn't bear looking at her with that expression on her face. "Nothing."

A guard holding a cup of coffee neared the door. He met Ian's gaze, then dropped the paper cup and reached for his firearm. "Freeze!" he said, long before freeing his gun and pointing it at him and Marie.

Marie's soft mouth opened into an "O."

Great. Now they had to worry about a trigger-happy NYPD Blue wanna-be.

Ian held up his hands. "The head nurse brought us in."

The guard looked dubious. He also looked more nervous than Ian was comfortable with, the gun twitching in his hands.

"Go ask her."

He didn't move, but he did look down the hall.

"Better yet, let me get her," Marie said, slowly reaching for the call button next to Nunzio's hand.

Within minutes the situation was entirely cleared up.

Well, almost entirely.

Ian stared at where the guard was talking to the nurse outside while an orderly cleaned up the puddle of coffee on the floor.

"I'm going to go call your dad," Ian quietly told Marie. And the Treasury agents. Something fishy was going on here and he wasn't going to be happy until he uncovered exactly where the smell was coming from.

THE FOLLOWING DAY Marie should have been ecstatic. Not only was her father completely cleared of any wrongdoing in Uncle Nunzio's accident, Uncle Nunzio himself had come out of his coma for a few minutes before she'd left his side at 4:00 a.m. He'd done little more than sputter and squeeze her hand before dropping off again, but the resident physician had assured her that was a very good sign, indeed.

Okay, so maybe she was tired. After all, she'd gotten little more than a couple of hours sleep on the sofa with her face smashed against a cheese puff. But as she sat in the conference room at noon listening to Jena and Dulcy and Barry discuss the ongoing search for a permanent secretary, she couldn't help thinking there was something more behind her curious lethargy. And that something was one very sexy, very provocative and very frustrating Ian Kilborn.

"Marie?"

She blinked several times, focused on her legal pad that held little more than unintelligible squiggles, then stared at Jena across the table. "Huh?"

Dulcy smiled at her. "What do you think about hiring Mrs. D'Onforio full-time?"

"Yes, um, that's fine," she said absently.

Jena sighed. "Uh-oh. Guy trouble at twelve o'clock."

Marie waved her away and turned the page of her legal pad. "There is no guy, so how can there be guy trouble?"

Jena and Dulcy shared a look.

Barry made a move to leave. "I think that's my cue to hightail it out of here before this love talk turns to me."

Marie waited for Jena to make a smart remark about Barry's bad handling of Mona, or Dulcy to frown at their older partner, but instead they both smiled at him like indulgent parents.

"Remember, Friday I need to see you to discuss that matter we talked about?" Dulcy asked him.

Suspicion briefly entered Barry's eyes. "Friday. Six o'clock. Right."

He left the room and immediately Jena and Dulcy turned to Marie.

But Marie had learned long ago that a good defense was an awesome offense. And in this case she had the perfect ammunition. "You can't seriously be considering going through with your off-the-wall plan, are you?"

"Of course we are," Jena said. "At six o'clock Friday night the three of us are going to fix what the two of them can't.''

The two of them being Barry and Mona.

Marie groaned and pushed her plate of cold cuts, veggies and fruit aside.

''Definitely guy problems,'' Jena said, watching the move.

Dulcy nodded. ''I haven't seen her eat a thing for three days.''

''What is it with you two and my eating habits. I...I happened to have a big breakfast this morning, that's all. Is that a criminal offense?''

Jena tilted her head and smiled a predatory smile. ''No. But not letting your friends in on what's going on between you and Ian Kilborn is.''

Marie caught her breath. ''Who told you? How did you find out? My God, how many other people know?''

''Relax, kiddo.'' Jena popped a red grape into her mouth. ''Not even Dulcy here had a clue until now.''

Dulcy's surprised expression told Marie that much was true.

''As to how I know, surely by now you've figured out that I know everything going on around the court-house.''

''How?''

''I have my sources.'' She wiped her fingers to-gether. ''And as for how many other people know, my guess would be no one. I haven't heard one tidbit of gossip about either one of you in legal circles. Well, aside from what's circulating about your father, that is.''

Dulcy put her notes in her briefcase. ''Thank God, everything's all right there.''

Marie leaned forward. "Where did you hear it, Jena?"

Her friend rolled her eyes and sighed. "All right, all right. If you're going to be bratty about it, I'll tell you. From Ian's ex-roommate."

Marie's skin grew so hot she was afraid she might faint.

"You see, this roommate went out with an old classmate of mine the other night. Tommy and I met them for drinks. And he proceeded to tell this completely inappropriate story about Ian's having brought a girl named Marie something-Italian home the other night and—"

Marie nearly sprang from her chair. "I get the picture. That's enough."

Jena's grin was decidedly catty. "Funny, that's what my friend told this guy, but he wouldn't be thwarted." She twisted her lips. "I only hope that Ian's better than his ex-roommate. Because this one was a complete jerk and a half."

Marie shrugged. "Never met him."

Which was true enough. She never had met Ian's roommate. As for the rest of what happened that night...well, she made a note to remind herself how very small the world was. The next thing she'd find out was her mother's best friend had seen her coming out of Room 7 of the motel before it burned to the ground.

She resisted the urge to bang her forehead against the conference table.

Dulcy pushed her plate closer to her. "Food really will help, Marie. Try to eat something. For me."

Marie gazed at her friend. Five months pregnant and

she still thought of everyone else first. She offered a small smile. Dulcy would make a great mother.

She picked up a piece of cheese and popped it into her mouth. Surprisingly, it didn't taste like the sawdust she feared, but smooth and tantalizing. She realized her appetite was making a slow comeback and she was immensely grateful. She fingered over the items on her plate and picked up a finger sandwich.

"And regarding Ian..." Dulcy began.

Marie groaned, her mouth full of ham, tomato and bread. "Oh, no, not you too."

"No, no, I'm not going to try to pry, Marie. I remember how things were with Quinn and I in the beginning... Anyway, I just want to say that if you want the guy, well, you owe it to yourself to go all out to get him." She looked down at where she was absently running her hands over her softly rounded belly and smiled. "If I could get up onto a stage and strip for Quinn like I did..." She glanced up again, complete bliss shining from her face. "Well, you get the picture."

Jena made a sound of objection and rolled her eyes to stare at the ceiling. "Oh, thanks, Dulc. Just what I needed. An image of a pregnant you in a bikini gyrating for dollars."

Dulcy playfully nudged Jena's arm and laughed. "I gyrated for love. And it's what got me pregnant, mule." She sat back. "Just you wait, Jena. Your date with the child bug is coming up fast."

Jena pulled a face. "Not in this lifetime."

Marie cupped a hand to her mouth and said to Dulcy, "Wouldn't it be funny if she's the one who ends up with ten kids?"

"That doesn't even near funny," Jena said, giving

a visible shudder. She waved her hand. "Anyway, enough about me." She leaned forward with a completely scheming expression on her classically pretty face. "Let's map out exactly what we're going to do to Barry and Mona this Friday."

14

ALL'S WELL THAT ENDS WELL.

Ian handed a cup of coffee to Frankie Sr. then joined him on the bench across the street from the U.S. Treasury Department. He frowned at his own lame statement. Sure, while everything was looking good for Frankie Bertelli Sr., he wasn't so sure "well" could apply to his and Marie's messy end.

"Coffee?" Frankie Sr. asked.

Ian nodded.

Funny, but for the first time in his life he didn't care about the reporters gathered in front of the Treasury Department waiting for him and Frankie Sr. to exit. Instead, they'd gone out the back, then made their way to the coffee shop around the corner. The reporters' attention was focused on the front doors of the building, no one catching on that their targets sat a mere fifty feet behind them.

What did that mean? Normally he would have at least stepped into the spotlight of media attention himself. After all, it wasn't so much success that made a career but the perception of success. And having your face and your comments all over the television news and print media definitely helped in that perception. He glanced at Frankie Sr. And this, by far, had been the case with the highest stakes of his life—at least where scandal was concerned.

"Local Dry Cleaner Suspected of Laundering More Than Clothes," the headlines had read for the past two weeks, along with pictures of him and Frankie Sr. The mere hint that mafia existed in Albuquerque was enough to keep all forms of the media buzzing.

Strangely, though, he hadn't taken on the case for its high profile. He'd taken it on because Frankie Sr. was Marie's father and because he'd grown up down the street from the Bertellis. And that, alone, was so unlike the old Ian that...

What was he thinking? "Old" Ian? The guy he saw in the mirror every morning, who greeted the senior partners at the firm as a confident up-and-comer, was the same guy he'd always been.

Okay, maybe not exactly the same. The old Ian might have milked the media attention for all it was worth and nabbed the partnership position he'd been jockeying for since coming back home. The old Ian would never have missed the warning signs his roommate had given off for the past week and booted him out before he'd had a chance to steal him blind. The old Ian would be ecstatic about the successful outcome of his case.

The old Ian wouldn't have cared if a woman had walked out on him.

He rubbed the back of his neck. But if there was an old Ian, then that meant there also had to be a new one. If that was the case, who in the hell was he? And how, exactly, did he boot *him* out?

Because facts were facts. And while, yes, he admitted to having undergone some changes during his brief time with Marie, he couldn't even think the word "marriage" without feeling physically ill. He slid Frankie Sr. a glance. And that reaction didn't have anything to do with the inevitability of physical injury should Marie's family find out about them.

Frankie Sr. caught his gaze and grinned. "How do you take yours?"

"Take my what?"

Frankie gestured toward his cup. "Your coffee."

Ian squinted at the older man through the bright, late-afternoon sunlight. They'd just come from a grueling three-hour meeting with the agents from hell and the man was asking him how he took his coffee?

He shrugged. What was the harm in answering? "Four sugars, lots of cream."

"Ah. A man of indulgences."

Ian cracked a smile. "I guess you could say that." He shifted on the bench. The February day was warm, but not all that warm and the bench was hard and cold. "Don't you think that you and I should be talking about what just happened in the building across the street?"

Frankie Sr. looked at the building in question and eyed the reporters milling about in front of it. "What's there to talk about? They were trying to bring down Jimmy Baldacci in Chicago and they thought the way to do that was to frame me."

Ian stared at him.

A lesser man would be furious at what the Treasury agents had pulled. Hell, Ian was majorly upset. Essentially, the entire case against Frankie Bertelli Sr. had been a scam. Basically, it was a sting of sorts designed to get him to testify against his friend Jimmy the Head, the mobster Marie called Uncle Jimmy. The agents all but admitted having known all along that Frankie hadn't done away with Nunzio, simply because they'd known where Nunzio was, namely in the ICU ward.

They had even put a round-the-clock guard on him to keep his identity a secret. Which was why Ian's firm's detectives hadn't been able to check the identity of the John Doe that had been admitted to the hospital two weeks ago. And Nunzio's unconscious state had only made their job to keep him under wraps easier.

Ian absently sipped his coffee. He had to hand it to the agents, though. They had acted swiftly the moment news of Nunzio's accident had come over the airwaves. It seemed they'd been trying to work an angle for months to pull Frankie in and their agents had been first on Nunzio's accident scene on I-40. They'd stripped the unwitting, injured accountant of his identification and lifted the "missing" books that supposedly implicated Frankie Sr. in an elaborate money-laundering scheme, and set in motion a plan to get Frankie to rat out one of his oldest friends, who just happened to be a real, honest-to-God mobster.

"The SOBs didn't even apologize," Ian said quietly, warming his hands against his cup.

"They never do."

Ian frowned and eyed the older Italian. "You sound like you speak from experience."

Frankie's dark eyes sparkled in the late-afternoon sunlight. "Maybe because I am." He stretched out his arm and rested it back against the bench. "Then again, maybe I'm not."

Ian pointed a finger at him. "You know, it's talk like that makes everyone wonder if you really are mafia."

Frankie shrugged. "It's not what everyone thinks. It's what everyone can prove."

Ian stared at him. This whole on-again, off-again roller-coaster ride concerning Frankie's true loyalties was making Ian a little green about the gills. "So, Frankie. Are you...affiliated?"

"Tell me, counselor. How, exactly, would you advise me to answer that question?"

Ian felt a tremendous amount of respect grow inside him...along with nausea. "Point taken."

"Now," Frankie said, taking a long sip from his coffee. "Back to your indulgences..."

Ian's spine snapped upright. Indulgences? Who was talking about indulgences?

Frankie Sr. shook a finger at him. "It's a woman, no? A woman who has you distracted?"

Ian smoothed down his tie. "I'm not distracted. Hey, I was focused enough to save your ass from frying."

Frankie chuckled. "The truth would have come out sooner or later. I'm just glad it came out now, you know, before I spent a few nights in jail." He motioned toward Ian's suit. "You're wrinkled. Your hair is barely combed. You look like you haven't slept for days. Distracted. Very definitely distracted."

"My clothes aren't pressed because my ex-roommate took my iron." And his ironing board, and just about everything else in his apartment.

"Your clothes aren't pressed because a woman climbed into your head and won't get out."

A couple of white-collar workers walked by clutching briefcases, their attention on the media mob across the street. Ian absently watched them. "I suppose that's one way of putting it."

He rubbed his chin. Was he really sitting there on a bench talking to Marie's father about...well, her?

Of course, Frankie had no idea that's who they were discussing, but when all was said and done, that's what was happening, wasn't it? And considering Frankie's cagey answers to the mafia question, Ian wasn't too sure he wanted to pursue this conversation any further. In fact, he was convinced of it.

Besides, there was nothing left to discuss, was there? He and Marie had a white-hot affair that ended when she walked out on him the other night. Nothing more, nothing less.

His mind wandered toward questions and what-ifs that he didn't want to follow. What if he'd gone after her that night? What if he'd grabbed her and kissed her last night when she'd come to the hospital, like he'd wanted to? What if he'd shown up on her doorstep and refused to leave until she saw him?

What if, what if, what if.

God, he'd never hated two words more in his life.

Frankie patted his knee. The sudden, hearty movement made Ian jump. He steadied his cup, then shook droplets of coffee from his fingers.

Frankie made a sound of approval. "A party. Yes. That's what we need. A party to celebrate the end of all this nonsense."

Ian's brows rose. "A party?"

"Yes. A Bertelli party." He narrowed his eyes. "You ever been to one?"

Ian nodded slightly. "I went to Frankie Jr.'s college graduation party." It's also where he had cornered Marie in the kitchen pantry and, up against a rope of garlic, had his way with her.

He squinted. Or had she had her way with him?

"Well, then, you must come to this one, too. This Saturday night."

"Saturday night…" Ian tried to come up with a plausible reason why he couldn't make it.

"You'll be there. Six o'clock. We'll start out with a

nice dinner and go from there. Maybe I'll bring in music.''

''Music…''

Frankie Sr. grinned. ''Yes, a party. A party in your honor for helping me get through this…'' he motioned with his hand ''…garbage.''

Ian grimaced. Not only was Frankie Sr. throwing a party, he was throwing it for Ian. Which pretty much eliminated any plausible reason for wiggling out of the invite beyond death.

He froze.

That wasn't even funny.

Frankie Sr. cleared his throat. ''I, um, think we've been spotted.''

Ian glanced toward the throng of reporters. A cameraman with his lens pointed in the direction of the department doors was looking their way. His camera slowly followed his eyesight until he had them in his crosshairs.

Ian took his cell from his inside pocket and pressed a button. Across the street, other reporters had caught on to the lone cameraman and en masse they began hurrying across the four-lane boulevard, oblivious to the rush-hour traffic and the loud honking of horns. The first of them were just about to reach the curb when a long, black limo cut off their progress and pulled up to the curb.

Ian stood up and took Frankie Sr.'s arm. ''That would be your ride, Frankie.''

''My ride? But I didn't order a limo.''

Ian grinned. ''No. I did.''

He hurried the older man to where the driver already had the back door open. Frankie climbed inside and Ian glanced in at him.

"A party. That's exactly what you need."

Ian grinned as he closed the door then turned to do his job.

THAT FRIDAY NIGHT, the ladies' plans were under way at the law office of Lomax, Ferris, McCade and Bertelli.

"You've got to keep Barry occupied," Jena said urgently as the clock ticked toward six.

Marie glanced around the dark, quiet waiting room and wondered why they were whispering. You'd think it was midnight and that they'd just broken in, when, in fact, they'd officially knocked off work an hour ago and the sun was just setting.

"What? Me?" she asked, about a breath away from full-blown panic. "And just how do I do that?"

Jena was looking at her watch then craning her neck to see out into the hall. "The building should be empty now, but I'll make sure on my way out."

"And what are you going to do about the security guards?"

Jena stared at her. "They only make perimeter checks, Marie."

"I know that. But what about the alarms?" She waved to the console near the front door. "Surely, they'll think to trip those."

"Ah, woman of little faith." Jena linked her arm with Marie's, then began leading her to Barry's office. "I disarmed those this morning when I came in."

She should have known.

They stopped outside Barry's door and Jena released her arm. Marie instantly latched onto her friend. "Wait!" she whispered. "Dulcy's in there now. Why not let her keep Barry busy?"

"What? And let you help me with Mona?" Jena shook her head. "Mona would see through you in ten seconds flat, Marie."

Marie made a face and crossed her arms. "And what about Barry?"

"He already thinks you're a little spacey so he probably won't question your obvious agitation."

"Spacey?"

Jena grinned, then gave Marie a shove toward the door. "Don't worry. It works in our favor."

Oh, that helped a lot.

Marie righted herself and found that she was standing directly in the doorway of Barry's office. She nervously straightened her skirt, cursing Jena's accurate shove.

Forget that her father and her sister-in-law Toni could have ended up in the slammer. When this night was done, she would probably turn out to be the only Bertelli in jail.

"Marie!" Dulcy said, rising from where she sat at the edge of a plush black leather sofa. Barry rose along with her from a chair next to Dulcy.

"Um, yeah," Marie said dumbly. "Hi."

Oh, she was so not good at this.

She stared at Barry to see if he was suspicious but found him unsurprised by her behavior. Oh, great. Jena was right. He did think she was spacey.

Marie cleared her throat. "I'm sorry, I didn't mean to interrupt. But since you're still here, Barry, I'd hoped I could ask your advice about something." She looked between him and her friend. "But I can come back if you two are busy." She began backing toward the door.

"No," Dulcy said a little too sharply, earning a curious glance from Barry. "Actually, Barry and I were just finishing. Weren't we, Barry?"

"Sure. If you say so." He scratched his head, then smoothed back his thick white hair. "I suppose I can spare a minute or two, Marie." He glanced at his watch.

Dulcy gave him a kiss on both cheeks then a quick hug. "Thanks, Barry. I appreciate your listening to me."

"Anytime, darlin'."

Marie frowned as Dulcy made a beeline for the door, giving Marie a long warning look as she passed.

Marie suppressed the desire to shout, "What?"

So she wasn't any good at deception. She, for one, tended to count that as a very good thing.

Dulcy finally left the room. If either Marie or Barry found the fact that she'd closed the door behind her unusual, neither of them said anything. Instead Marie stood there feeling ten kinds of a fool trying to pinpoint the exact moment Barry had labeled her as spacey and wondering how she was supposed to keep him busy for an unspecified period of time.

Barry cleared his throat and motioned toward the couch. "Have a seat, Marie."

"Seat? Oh, yeah. Sure. Thanks." She crossed to the sitting area and sank down into the buttery soft leather. If the scent reminded her a little too much of her dark crossing through Ian's living room, she wasn't going to admit it.

"You wanted my advice on something, you said?" Barry prompted her, sitting on the edge of his own seat.

Marie had always liked the older attorney. He was attractive and gregarious and genuinely seemed to like people. And his grin made her feel…safe somehow.

She fidgeted. She'd better watch it or she'd end up lying back on the sofa and confessing all. She ran her hand absently over the soft leather, thinking this was very much what a psychologist would have in his or her office. The mere act of sitting on it made her want to explore her psyche, vent her most secret emotions, and admit that she loved a man who was emotionally incapable of loving her back.

"Um, yes. I did," she said in delayed response. "You see, there's this ongoing issue with my father..."

Marie found herself sinking further into the sofa and feeling much too comfortable than was emotionally safe.

Was Dulcy right? Had she thrown in the towel with Ian too early? After all, she hadn't even given him a chance to explain himself. She gave a mental shrug. Then again, he hadn't appeared all that interested in explaining anything anyway, given the way he'd essentially run from the bedroom for the kitchen to nuke frozen pizza.

The image of him standing in the middle of the parking lot, sans towel made her smile.

Barry's chair creaked as he recrossed his legs. "From what I understand your father is well out of the woods."

Marie blinked at him as if surprised to find him still there. "Oh. Yes. Yes, he is, thank you." She forced herself to sit up or else the next thing she knew she'd be exploring the possibility of past lives transgressions and how they impacted her present life.

Hmm...were she and Ian ceaselessly destined to come together, then part again? God, she hoped not. But the idea of fate helped justify the humongous ache that had taken up residence in her heart the night she left him. An ache that had exponentially intensified when she saw him at the hospital the other night.

Marie bunched her hands into fists. It wasn't fair this, this…longing for a man who would have had Bachelor Forever tattooed across his chest, if he went in for that sort of thing. He'd used her twice now, then moved on as if remembering her name hadn't even been important.

"Actually, Barry, what I wanted to talk to you about has nothing to do with my father."

He frowned and glanced at his watch.

Marie sat up even straighter. "You see, there's a question I've been dying to ask you but haven't dared to…until now."

After a long silence, he sighed. "And that question is?"

If Barry had been her father, he would have been gesturing for her to hurry it up. But Barry wasn't her father. He was Barry. Dear, sweet, twisted, socially repressed Bartholomew Lomax.

"Yes," she said. "My question is…why in the hell didn't you marry Mona when you had the chance?"

Barry made a choking sound. Marie crossed her arms to wait him out…only the bout went on longer than she was comfortable with.

Oh, geez, she'd gone and killed the guy.

She rushed to his side and heartily patted his back. "What is it? Are you okay? Oh, God, Barry, I don't think I can handle this on top of everything else right now."

He was motioning toward something on his desk. Marie hurried to collect the glass of water there, then helped him drink from it. He tried to motion her away, but she wouldn't hear of it.

After long moments of sipping, coughing and deep breaths, finally Barry's colored returned to normal. His fit had slowed to a quiet throat clearing and he'd drained the contents of his water glass. Marie stepped to refill it from an ice pitcher on a side bureau, then handed it to him.

"Thanks," he said.

Marie smiled. "It's not every day someone thanks me for nearly killing them."

Barry cracked a smile. "It's not every day that someone is as brutally honest with their questions as you are, Marie." He put his glass down on top of the antique coffee table as she retook her seat. "I don't know if I ever told you, but I watched you in court once."

Marie grimaced. "Recently?"

He shook his head. "No. Last year, when Dulcy first approached me with the idea of taking the three of you on with me here."

"You flew to L.A.?"

"Yes. It was a big risk Dulcy was asking me to take and I wanted to be sure it was a sound one." Barry smoothed down his tie. "In the case I watched you prosecute I'd basically surmised that the defense was going to win." He grinned at her. "Then you got up and gave the defendant such a verbal beating he could barely walk a straight line when you got done with him."

Marie looked down at her folded hands. Maybe she should have given one of those to Ian. Strangely enough, she hadn't even opened her mouth. Such a strong verbal advocate in court, she'd lost her voice when it came to matters of the heart. In fact, the past three weeks emerged as some sort of aberration of sorts. It had begun with her feeling restless with her love life and her life as a whole. Where she'd previously drawn on her strength as a competent, successful attorney, she'd lost even the ability to do that. Almost as if fate was telling her that until she figured the rest of it out, nothing would go smoothly.

Barry continued, jarring her from her thoughts. "I was so impressed I called Dulcy right from the courtroom after the judge had made her decision. In your favor, no less."

She cleared her throat. "And what did you to tell her?"

"The deal was on."

Marie felt oddly flattered that he'd made his decision based solely on watching her in court. And that her recent behavior hadn't affected his overall opinion of her as a proficient attorney.

She also felt a little disappointed that he'd avoided her question. "Well, um, thank you for that, Barry. I'm very glad everything worked out. I got to come home and…" She smiled at him. "And you didn't answer my question."

His answering grin was bigger, although there was a smear of pain and sadness in his gray eyes. "I know."

"You're not going to either, are you?"

"If it's all the same to you…no, I'm not."

Marie nodded. "Fair enough." She wasn't sure how she would have reacted had *he* had asked *her* a question about her love life.

What his answer did allow, however, was a measure of relief.

She smiled. Maybe, just maybe, she, Jena and Dulcy were doing the right thing after all.

"I'M SO SORRY!" MARIE said a few minutes later, right after she'd "accidentally" dumped the entire contents of Barry's water glass in his lap. "Oh, God." She grabbed the small pile of napkins from the bureau, made to blot the growing stain, then handed the napkins to him instead. "We're, um, going to need more. Let me go get some."

She rushed through the door, then closed it after herself, her heart racing. This wasn't going to work. There was no way it was going to work. She started toward the conference room to see if Mona had arrived for Dulcy's fake baby shower yet only to run into Jena coming out.

"I was just coming to get you," Jena whispered, tugging her away from the doorway.

"Good, because I don't think I could have stood another moment in there."

"Come on." Jena peeked into the conference room where Marie heard Dulcy and Mona talking, then made a dash for the door.

"But Dulcy—"

"Dulcy's going to join us in a minute. Hurry up, before Barry comes out of his office."

"And Mona?"

Jena grinned. "Mona thinks she's early and is helping set up the food she thinks is for the guests. Of course, it's meant to keep her and Barry over the weekend."

"Ah." She'd known they were leaving food. And when Mona and Barry checked, they would also find soft bedding, pillows, candles and, of course, wine stocked in the supply closet. Dulcy had even thought to provide clothes for both of them.

It was a well laid-out plan that, with any luck, would have the results they wished for.

Marie and Jena rushed through the outer door and ducked off to either side, taking turns keeping an eye out for Dulcy.

"Here she comes!" Marie whispered.

And there she was. Dulcy hurried from the conference room and cut a path straight for the door. Within a matter of moments, the three of them stood on the other side of the double locked barrier waiting for the moment of truth on the other side.

Marie's heart skipped a beat as she watched Barry's office door open.

Dulcy gasped. "What did you do to him?" she asked as all three stared at the wet spot on the front of his pants.

"Knock it off. It's only water," Marie said. Her friends stared at her. She shrugged. "It was all I could think of with such short notice."

Barry hadn't spotted them yet. Instead he was busy going through the temp's desk, presumably looking for more paper towels. He must have heard a sound because he headed for the conference room instead…just as Mona came out of it.

They stood for long moments staring at each other, then in unison looked toward the door where the three of them stood grinning.

Jena waggled her fingers. "Bye, guys," she shouted. "Have a nice weekend. We'll see you first thing Monday morning."

Marie giggled as she followed Jena down the steps, Dulcy on her heels. Their laughter mingled with the banging of fists against the reinforced plate-glass door.

15

ONLY HER FAMILY WOULD think of throwing a party to celebrate *not* being arrested. But then, her parents thought any occasion was excuse enough to have a party.

She methodically sliced up celery sticks at the kitchen island while her mother checked one of the three sauces boiling on the industrial stove behind her and her grandmother checked fresh bread baking in the oven. Near the gigantic table, her sister-in-law Toni tried to supervise her and Frankie Jr.'s two children while she constructed tiramisu. Marie had learned that Frankie Jr. was staying at their parents' house. After spending a night at a motel room he'd finally given in and confessed all to Ma, probably hoping she would then turn around and chew out Marie for having kicked him out. Oh, Marie had suffered through a full-blown Francesca fit over the phone the other day. But it had been because she hadn't gone to her mother the minute Frankie Jr. showed up on her doorstep, not for the reasons Frankie Jr. had hoped.

Marie covertly wiped a smile from her face. From what she could tell, Frankie Jr. was suffering a fate worse than death being back home, and she heard tell that at least three times a day he begged Toni to take him back.

She frowned. Of course, Toni wasn't talking to Marie either after what went down at Little Italia. She reminded herself that it didn't matter. It was her brother's family that was important in the end. And she was already entertaining ways to help them back together even as she chopped.

Of course, knowing that Barry and Mona were locked up in the firm's office together for the weekend wasn't helping matters. She'd wanted to call, but Jena had seen to disconnecting the phone service as well. Something about an eager-to-please telephone repairman and vague promises she would never act on now that she was a married woman.

Marie really didn't want to know.

But she did hope that their little plan didn't jump and bite them all on the butt. After all, Barry didn't have the reputation as the best litigating attorney for nothing. If he pressed charges....

Perish the thought.

Marie's mother sidled up next to her, wiping her hands on her apron, a swatch of cloth with an outline of Sicily stitched into the smooth linen. "Two stalks, Marie. I asked for two stalks." She picked up the core of the fresh bunch of celery. "Waste. That's all you kids do is waste things." She turned and tossed the core into the sink. "Doesn't matter what. Food, marriages, love. That's all you do is waste."

Marie turned her head to stare at her mother, but she didn't seem aware that anyone had heard her as she piled things from the refrigerator into Marie's arms.

The guests had already begun arriving, but Marie was putting off leaving the kitchen to mingle. She hoped she might be able to get away with it all night.

She pushed the celery pieces into a mammoth bowl, then started in on the iceberg lettuce. The kitchen door opened and she jumped. But it wasn't frustratingly handsome Ian Kilborn who entered, but her brother Frankie Jr.

She rested the back of her knuckles against her thudding chest.

Frankie Jr. appeared decidedly awkward as he looked everywhere but at his wife, although his words were obviously directly toward her. He cleared his throat. "Cousin Gina is here with her three kids. She's taking all those under eight back to our old room, you know, to look after them."

Toni stared at him, her face drawn into tight lines.

Marie heard her mother mutter something in Italian behind her.

As if on cue, Gina came into the kitchen and rounded up Frankie Jr.'s two additions to what they always referred to as the "kids' room." Within moments she and the munchkins were gone, leaving five very silent adults behind.

Marie stared at her brother, silently urging him to say something, and her mother to remain quiet.

"Um, I guess I'd better get back out there."

Not exactly what Marie was hoping for.

"Fine," Toni said icily.

Not exactly the right response.

Marie smacked her knife against the cutting board, earning her the attention of everyone in the room.

"Oh, will you two just grow up already?" she shouted.

Everyone looked at her in surprise. And somewhere beneath all her frustration even Marie was a little shocked by her behavior as well. This was usually where her mother came in, ranting and raving and trying to force her opinion on everyone else. Marie had certainly never done anything like this.

Until now.

Marie rounded the corner, not stopping until she stood between the separated couple. "You," she pointed at Toni. "Apologize to Frankie."

Toni's face turned twenty shades of red. "Me? Why should I—"

Marie held up a hand to ward off the words. "Trust me, Toni, you don't have to say anything. We all know your point of view. Thoroughly. Lord knows we've all heard it enough." Now she held her hand up to her head. "And we've all had it up to here with it." She dropped her hand and leaned closer to her spitfire sister-in-law, distantly knowing she was putting herself within hitting range, but not caring. "We all know Frankie Jr. loves you and those kids more than anything in the world."

"But—"

"Shh," Marie said. "Let me finish."

Toni crossed her arms over her chest. Which was good, because it meant it would take some doing for her to uncross them and knock Marie on her butt.

Marie spoke evenly. "We also all know that he's not doing his secretary, Lola—no matter what the woman looks like." She narrowed her eyes. "And you know it too, Toni."

Her sister-in-law stared at her defiantly for a few moments, then all fight drained from her eyes and she looked away, her stance relaxing.

"Does that mean I'm right?" Marie asked.

Toni said something under her breath.

"Pardon me? I didn't hear you."

Toni's eyes snapped up. "Yes, it means you're right."

Frankie Jr. punched the air in triumph.

Marie turned her attention on him. "Oh, no, big brother. Now is definitely not the time to be celebrating. Because you haven't won anything here. Not yet."

The grin bled from his handsome face.

Marie poked her finger into his wide chest. "If you had been any kind of husband, your wife would never have suspected you of messing around on her. She would have been secure in your love for her and probably would have taken Lola out to lunch herself her first week on the job."

"But—"

"No buts, buster. Admit it. You do a piss-poor job as a husband. As the owner of a construction company, you excel. As a father, you're beyond compare. But as a husband...well, let's just say that there's something left to be desired."

She glanced at Toni to find her staring at the floor, her expression soft and hurt.

Frankie seemed to notice as well. "Aw, hell, Toni. You know I love you."

She blinked up at him, her brown eyes swimming in tears.

Marie discreetly backed up so the two were facing each other.

"Do I?" Toni asked. "When's the last time you told me, Frankie? Really showed me? You didn't even put up a fight when I asked you to move out. You just...just left."

"Oh, baby," Frankie said, looking more than a little choked up himself. "Come here."

By the time her brother had wrapped his wife up in

his colossal embrace, Marie had joined her mother and grandmother on the other side of the island. Her mother moved to stand on one side of her, her grandmother the other. It was obvious the couple across the room no longer knew anyone else was there as they spoke in quiet whispers, then finally stepped out the back door together and walked toward the gazebo at the back of the property.

Marie looked at her mother and grandmother, finding them both grinning at her.

"What?"

Her mother was the first to speak as she shook her head. "Our little Marie has finally become a woman."

She made a face, even though there was a small spark of pride in her chest. "I became a woman a long time ago. You just didn't notice. What happened now is that your little Marie lost her temper. She probably would have been better off keeping her mouth shut."

After several long moments of silence, the three of them returned back to the meal preparations. If anyone noticed the secret smiles they shared, they didn't say anything. It was enough for Marie to know that after years of kicking and screaming and rebelling to prove herself, she finally shared the connection she'd been yearning for with her mother and grandmother—a connection that transcended mere blood ties. They were now connected through mutual respect.

EVERY INCH OF IAN'S SKIN itched. He'd been in the Bertelli house for twenty minutes meeting and greeting what seemed like dozens of family members, and throughout he'd tried like hell not to scratch. Maybe he was coming down with something. Or maybe he'd stumbled into a patch of poison ivy or something.

It was February 14th. Valentine's Day. There wasn't any poison ivy.

He caught himself raking at his arm through his lightweight black sweater. Or was there? He made a face. It had to be something and poison ivy sounded like a good explanation. At least as good a one as he was willing to fess up to. There was no way he was going to admit his condition might be a result of seeing Marie in her family environment.

"Wool?"

"Hmm?" Ian looked to find Marie's brother Anthony addressing him.

Anthony pointed to the sweater. "Wool always makes me itch like hell. First Ma used to make me wear it all the time, and now it seems it's all Connie brings home for me."

Ian watched Anthony scratch his own arm through his wool sweater and thought about telling Marie's brother that it was all right for a guy to shop for himself nowadays. He didn't, of course, because he didn't think Anthony would get it anyway. The Bertellis were a very traditional family in which men didn't shop and women bought their men wool sweaters and expected them to wear them.

Then again, the thought of Marie rubbing lotion on him after the event definitely had its plus points.

His shoulders stiffened. What was he thinking? Marie was barely even talking to him, much less offering to scratch his itch. In more ways than one.

"The man of the hour," Frankie Sr. boomed then slapped Ian so hard on the back he completely forgot about all types of itches and instead concentrated on keeping breakfast down. He smiled at the oldest member of the Bertelli family and lifted his tumbler of cognac.

"To Frankie Bertelli Sr.," he called out.

There were echoes of "salute" all around the living room and dining room, and even out onto the front porch, as everyone toasted their host.

Frankie squeezed his shoulder and moved him toward the corner of the room. "What, no date?" he asked, looking around for a woman.

"No, no date. Um, too short of notice."

Ian cringed. He hadn't even thought about that. Which was probably a good thing because Lord only knew how Marie would have reacted to that. His guess was not very well. He'd heard the story about Frankie Jr.'s wife Toni and his secretary at Little Italia. Marie probably would have made that look like a minor misunderstanding had he brought another woman into her family's house.

But knowing that and understanding that were two completely different things. Ian didn't understand why he felt confident she'd take some kind of possessive action if another woman were involved when she'd made it clear she wanted nothing to do with him.

He looked up to find Frankie Sr. grinning at him in a way that made him itch all over again.

"You're looking distracted again," the older man said.

Ian glanced at his clothes. He'd taken extra care to make sure they were pressed and that his hair was nicely combed, his face shaven. He found everything in place. "I'm, um, not used to such large gatherings," he said.

Oh, boy, was that ever the wrong thing to say. If anyone knew just how large his own family was, and how huge their family gatherings were, it would be Frankie Bertelli. Hadn't his family just lived down the street from them while he was growing up? Hadn't there always been jokes about the Kilborn girls marrying the Bertelli boys? The punch line had been that none of them would ever leave the neighborhood but instead would go on to populate the whole of Albuquerque with Bertellis.

He realized what he'd just been thinking and grimaced.

"If you'll excuse me, Frankie, I think I need to get some air."

Frankie nodded. "Air. Yes. Maybe that will put some color back into your face."

Ian headed for the nearest door, only to find out too late it was the door to the kitchen and that inside stood the woman he'd been avoiding for the past hour.

Marie.

Aw, hell.

MARIE DROPPED THE KNIFE she was holding and stared at the man she'd been looking for all night.

Okay, she hadn't exactly been looking for him as in she'd combed the house and watched through the windows for his car. But every time someone opened the kitchen door, her heart had skipped a beat and she'd half expected him to be standing there.

And now that he was, she didn't know quite what to do.

She wiped her hands on her slacks. She did know one thing. She wished he would stop looking at her that way. As if afraid she might be tempted to launch the knife in front of her at him.

She cleared her throat. "Hi," she said, figuring she owed that much to her father's guest of honor.

"Yes, um, hi."

Marie looked around. All the dinner preparations were done—the burners were turned off, the oven set to warm, the salad chilling in the crisper. Her mother and grandmother had left the room five minutes ago to mingle a bit before setting everything out.

The kitchen was empty except for her and Ian.

If the scene reminded Marie a little too much of the scenario from eight years ago…well, she wasn't going to go there. She was no longer a teen with a crush. But Ian was very definitely still the cool neighborhood boy who had a way of talking her out of her underwear.

She shifted as if checking to make sure they were still in place. Yep. And that's where they were going to stay.

Ian gestured toward the door with his thumb. "Your family sure knows how to throw a party."

"Mmm," she answered. Which was a nonanswer, really, because what he'd said really hadn't been a question. Rather, it had been lame commentary that demanded little more than a lame response.

Marie turned away from him and slid her knife into the dishwasher. "What are you doing here, Ian?"

She heard him clear his throat, the sound revealing he was closer than he'd been a moment before. "I'm the guest of honor."

Marie pretended to be busy clearing off the cutting board, stuffing the vegetable remains down the trash compactor. "That's not what I meant." She turned toward him. "I meant, what are you doing in here? In the kitchen?"

Marie's breath caught in her throat when she found

him not only closer, but dangerously so. She'd noticed he looked irresistible in his close-fitting black sweater and black slacks when he'd entered the room, but now she smelled him, too. And the combination of sight and smell was wrecking double havoc on her senses.

He gave her a half cocky, half uncertain smile. "You know what today is, don't you?"

Marie heard herself swallow. "The day of my father's party?"

He worked his fingers partway up one of his sweater sleeves and pulled out a single cellophane-wrapped rose.

Valentine's Day.

Marie felt suddenly dizzy. She had been so wrapped up in the mess that was currently her life, she had completely forgotten. How, she didn't know, since everywhere you looked, everywhere you went, there were red paper heart reminders and love songs on the radio.

Ian shook out the red, red rose. The sweet scent mingling with his one hundred percent manly scent nearly buckled her knees. "Will you be my valentine, Marie Bertelli?"

16

WHOA.

One minute Marie was looking at him like he was evil incarnate, the next she was kissing him like he was air and she was in desperate need of a breath.

Ian wrapped his arms around her. Oh, he was definitely not complaining. His fingers found her hips and he hauled her against him, molding her to his hard length.

And here he had thought the whole rose bit was hokey. That she'd laugh at him when he produced it from his sleeve. Instead, the simple gesture had netted him far more than he ever dreamed.

Marie made a soft sound in her throat and maneuvered him backward. A few steps later, he realized where she was leading him—to the same pantry where he had first sampled her sweet, hot wares some eight years before.

Good God…

This time, however, their roles were changed. Whereas *he'd* had *her* pushed up against the ropes of garlic back then, that's where *she* had *him* now. And she couldn't seem to get enough of him. Her hands shoved up his sweater and then fumbled with the front catch of his slacks, her calf bending around his as she ground her pelvis hungrily against his.

Ian moved his hands to either side of her face, stilling her head as he looked deep into her eyes in the dim light slanting in from the kitchen. There was no door to keep anyone in the back of the kitchen from seeing them. But the way they were ducked off to the side put them in shadow.

Marie restlessly licked her lips, the backs of her fingers sliding against his abdomen as she dove for the proof of his arousal. And, oh boy, did she ever find it, thick and hard and pulsing like hell with need for her.

"Kiss me," she whispered, eyeing his mouth.

His gaze raked her flushed features, but still he held her head still.

"I said kiss me, damn it," she said more forcefully, squeezing his erection to the point of pain.

And Ian did. He kissed her until her breathing came in ragged gasps. Until he thought he would lose it right then and there.

Until there was a sound in the kitchen.

Whoa.

But this time it wasn't a good kind of *whoa.*

Ian set Marie away from him.

"My grandmother," she whispered and tried to kiss him again.

Ian worked his hand between them and curved his fingers over her seeking mouth.

"I don't care if she knows," she murmured when he released her.

He eyed her in the dim light. "I do."

For long moments, they stood like that, listening to the sounds of spoons stirring and plates being stacked in the kitchen a few feet away.

Then Marie made a sound of utter and complete frustration and brought her foot down firmly on his instep.

She shook her finger in his face. "Don't you ever come near me again, do you hear me Ian Kilborn. Never."

Ian felt panic rise in his throat as he grasped her arm to keep her from leaving the pantry. He knew he'd been given an important second chance when she'd accepted his rose and welcomed his attentions. With her words, he also knew that she meant what she said. If he let her go now, he'd never have another chance again.

Her gaze was glued to his face, waiting for him to say something.

Ian heard Francesca Bertelli's voice, followed by Frankie Sr.'s, and an altogether different kind of panic swelled in him. He released Marie's arm. She glanced away from him. But before she did, he witnessed an expression so full of disappointment, of pain, that it made him hurt for her.

He leaned against the garlic ropes and swallowed hard, watching helplessly as the only woman he had ever loved walked out of his life for the second time.

THREE HOURS LATER, Marie stood outside the doors of Lomax, Ferris, McCade and Bertelli, Attorneys-at-Law, convinced that making someone fall in love with someone else was impossible. She rifled through her purse looking for her keys. If tears impeded her progress, she chose to ignore them…at least until she couldn't see, period.

Oh, boy.

She leaned a hand against the wall and tried to stem the flow. She hadn't known it was possible to love someone so much. She seemed to feel Ian with every cell of her being. When she breathed in, it was him she smelled. When she slept, it was him she dreamt of.

When she thought of something worthy of sharing with someone, it was him she wanted to tell.

She hadn't known how much she loved him until she was absolutely certain that he could never love her in the same way.

Damn, damn, damn. If this was her way of trying to get a grip, she was doing a piss-poor job of it. Rather than her keys, she pulled a pack of tissues out of her purse and set to work mopping up the mess that was her face.

Getting through dinner had been one of the toughest things she had ever done, especially when she realized that she and Ian had been placed next to each other in typical boy-girl-boy-girl succession around the large dining room table. Even when she wasn't looking, she was aware of every move he made. Could taste the food he put into his mouth. And felt like someone was squeezing the life out of her with every casual word he said to the other guests.

She, on the other hand, had been incapable of any speech. She'd hurried through the meal—tough to do when there were three courses of different pastas and no one was in a hurry to serve them—then excused herself and disappeared into the kitchen, presumably to see to the growing pile of dishes. Only the first chance she got, she slipped through the back door, climbed into her car, and ended up down here.

No, she thought, soaking the last of her tissues. You couldn't make someone love you if they didn't. And Ian didn't love her. It was as simple as that. And lust wasn't enough for her.

She blinked at the etched-glass door and the darkness beyond, almost forgetting where she was and what she planned to do. She cupped her hands against the

glass, trying to make out movement on the other side.
Had Barry and Mona found a way out? Surely not even
Jena could plan for every contingency. If they'd been
desperate enough, the star-crossed couple could have
found a way out through the ventilation system.

She finally found her keys and unlocked the two
locks on the door, then pushed the glass inward.

"Hello?" she softly called out.

She looked to her left then her right, hoping that
Barry and Mona would forgive her for having gone
through with such a harebrained idea. What had she
been thinking? Sure, Jena and Dulcy had been very
convincing, but what they had done was...wrong.

"Barry?" she said, stepping to his door and looking
inside. She spotted a blanket draped across the leather
couch and wineglasses and candles on the coffee table.
Her brows rose.

"Mona?" she called out, stepping to the unisex
bathroom. Empty. As were the supply closet, her office
and the offices of Jena and Dulcy. She stepped to open
the closed conference room door. Obviously they'd
found a way out. She looked through the opening to
her office and the sparkling night view of Albuquerque
beyond. Maybe they'd climbed down? She made a
face, unsure if any of the windows even opened.

She opened the conference room door.

Gasps sounded all around.

Marie soundly closed the door and leaned against it,
her hand over heart.

Holy shit.

Marie squeezed her eyes shut against the images
burnt into her retinas. Images of Barry lying across the
conference room table, buck naked, a thick comforter

under him, while a very naked—was that Mona?—rode him like the bad girl she apparently was.

Holy shit.

Marie dropped the keys and quickly picked them up. She hurried to leave, then backtracked. She put a hand up to knock, then with shaking hands opened the door an inch instead. "I, um, am going now. I just, you know, wanted to let you know that you guys are free to leave."

She began to close the door when Mona said, "Lock it back up."

Marie was sure she was hearing things. "What?"

"She said lock it back up, Marie," Barry said.

"Oh. Okay. I, um, will do that." She quickly closed the door, then cracked it open again. "Are you sure?"

"I've never been surer of anything in my life," she thought she heard Barry murmur followed by a soft gasp from Mona.

Marie slammed the door, then ran the whole way to the parking lot.

MARIE FELT AS IF SHE'D just run a twenty-mile marathon after all she'd been through that evening. Five minutes into the trip back to her apartment the shock had begun to abate, leaving behind the hollow knowledge that apparently she was the only one incapable of making a man love her.

"Oh, shut up," she muttered to herself. Already she was tired of the idea of a pity party, even though she had barely even started it yet. A good pity party should include lots of chocolate and cheese puffs, although the only whining that would be allowed was red wine. Crying, yes. But absolutely no whining. She hated whiners. Especially when the whiner was her.

But didn't whining fall under the heading of self-pity?

Okay, she'd rename it. A self-sympathy party. That's it. Compassion without the wretched moaning and groaning.

Well, at least she came away from all this with one important piece of knowledge. She now knew where things stood between her and Ian. No more wondering if there might have been anything more if only she had done this or said that differently. Their relationship, what there was of it, had run its course, leaving her with no doubt that they weren't meant to be together. A supercharged sexual attraction, that's all that existed between them. Well, from his side anyway. She was afraid that things had gotten very serious very quickly on her side. Anyway, from here on out she wouldn't permit herself any more fantasies of chance meetings or secret rendezvous in the shadows with the sexy fellow attorney. She'd had more than her share of them both and they had left her feeling…well, used, somehow. Which was odd because she'd surely done as much taking as giving. Maybe disappointed was more the word she was looking for. Because while she never consciously recalled doing it, her subconscious had been a busy little ant building sandcastles in the sky. Sandcastles with cute little sand picket fences. A sand dog in the sand yard. A couple of little sand children chasing after it.

She rolled her eyes to stare at the ceiling, then checked her mailbox, even though she'd already collected it earlier in the day. Pathetic, that's what she was. Sand children, for God's sake. At this point that's probably as close to the real thing as she was going to get.

"Oh, shut up," she muttered again, then began trudging up the stairs.

When did the physical ache stop? she wondered. When would she be able to draw a breath and not be afraid her ribs would collapse on her heart and she'd never be able to breathe again? A day? A week? A month? Her hand was clammy against the railing. She'd never been in quite this state before, so she couldn't say with any measure of certainty.

Maybe she'd give Dulcy a call, see if she could offer some advice.

"Marie?"

For the second time that night, she nearly leapt straight out of her skin. She'd just turned to ascend the second flight of stairs when Ian had said her name. Or at least she thought she heard him say her name. He rose from where he was sitting on the top step, realizing that he had very definitely said her name.

"How long have you been here?" she whispered, hating that her heart skipped with hope and that her body temperature notched up a couple of thousand degrees just being in the same building with him.

"Not, um, long," he said quietly.

She glanced down at the keys she held in her hand. Anywhere but at him. Because to look at him hurt too much.

She cleared her throat. "If you came over hoping to finish what we started at my parents' house..." she stared defiantly at him, "forget it."

He stepped back to allow her to climb the rest of the steps, his striking features cast in relief by the hall light behind him. "That's not why I'm here."

Marie concentrated on taking the steps in a no-nonsense, confident way when she was really afraid her knees would buckle and she'd topple down to the bottom. She pointed at him. "Please tell me you didn't come here to apologize."

His grin disappeared. Marie stifled a groan.

"Actually, I did—come here to apologize, I mean."

She gave in to the frustrated groan as she raised her hand. "Don't. I don't think I could handle that on top of everything else that happened tonight."

He squinted at her. "How do you mean?"

She stepped to her door, then turned to face him, separating her apartment key from the rest of them on her Winnie the Pooh key ring. "I wonder. Hmm. Could it have anything to do with the fact that your apologizing would mean that you weren't only sorry that you don't feel the way about me that I feel about you, but that you regret everything else that happened between us over the past three weeks?" She tapped her finger against her chin. "You tell me, Ian. Why wouldn't I want to hear that?"

His grin made a hesitant return. "Is that what you think I'm here to apologize about?"

She felt like she was dealing with a particularly slow child, which probably wasn't all that far from the truth. Because while on the outside Ian looked like every woman's dream man with his handsome good looks and come-hither grin, emotionally he was all of twelve and had just stopped believing in cooties.

Perhaps he still did believe in cooties. The type that once guys caught them, they ended up in the middle of sandcastles, with sand dogs and sand kids.

"That's not what I want to apologize for."

She hiked a brow. "Oh?"

He shook his head and slowly advanced on her. "No."

Marie swallowed thickly. Ian had the look in his eye that only meant one thing. That he wanted to have her and he wasn't going to stop until he did.

She flattened her palm against his chest, ignoring the trembling of her thighs and his predatory advance. Okay, so physically she still wanted him. *Tell me something else I didn't know,* she thought dryly. But emotionally…she needed far more than he was willing to give.

Marie shivered. While Ian wasn't touching her, and the only contact between them was a restraining hand against his broad, hard, yummy chest, she felt like he was caressing her all over.

"What I came here to apologize for," he murmured, his gaze traveling over her face then settling on her mouth, "is not finishing what we started."

Marie suddenly felt like crying. That's what he was here for. The sex. To bring to a "climax" the desire they had both stoked in her parents' pantry. "You shit."

He shook his head, his gaze unwavering as he sought and locked onto hers. "You're not getting me, Marie."

"What's not to get?" she asked.

"Shh."

He quieted her words with a brief but scorching kiss.

"You see, I'm sorry for not going forward with… this thing that exists between us until it reached its natural conclusion."

She caught her breath even as she struggled to latch onto reason. "Thing?"

His lips quirked. "For lack of a better word, yes."

"I think the word you're looking for is sex."

"Mmm." He toyed with a strand of her hair, then used it as a brush of sorts against the sensitive skin of her throat. "Yes. Sex. You see, that's what I convinced myself it was. Sex. Great sex. Mind-blowing sex. But just sex."

Heat shimmered through her veins, hardening her nipples, making her all wet and needy and weak.

"But that's not at all what's happened between us, is it, Marie?"

Her heart pitched to her feet then bounced back up again. "It's not?"

"Uh-uh."

With each word he said, his voice grew lower, more provocative, and skated across her nerve endings like the lightest, most tantalizing of touches.

"You see, it took a very wise man to make me realize that." He threaded his fingers through her hair and cupped the back of her head. "He said, 'A woman has crawled into your head and won't get out.'" He kissed her again. "Only he neglected to mention the heart part, Marie, but it was there just the same. The fact that once a woman sneaks past your defenses, turns your life upside down, parks her sexy little butt into your heart…well, there's no getting her out." His grin was downright naughty while his eyes held all the emotion that roiled at the same time in her own chest. "And that's where you are, Marie. In my head. In my heart." A frown briefly marred his face. "And I was so very, very stupid for not having realized that until now."

He loved her.

Marie's legs threatened to give out from beneath her, forcing her to lean back against her apartment door for support. She thought she heard a sound from the other side. But that was impossible. No one was there.

Frankie Jr. had finally gone back to his wife. And she didn't have any pets.

At least not yet. But that sand dog was looking more real with every heartbeat.

Marie restlessly licked her lips. This was progress. A step in the right direction. But what was to stop Ian from waking up in the morning and running from her again? Not physically, because *she* had been the one to do that to *him*—twice in fact—although for the opposite reason, namely because she had been ready to commit while he hadn't. No, what if he was to run from her emotionally? Decide that too much was at stake? Reerect the barriers that had kept him from coming this far? After all, very little had changed between them, aside from the words he'd just uttered.

"Marry me, Marie."

Her legs gave out.

"Whoa." Ian chuckled softly as he kept her from collapsing to the floor in a liquid puddle of desire and shock.

Tears burned the back of her eyelids as she fought to regain her bearings. "That's not even funny, Ian."

"Who's joking?"

She searched his face, trying to dig up one scrap of uncertainty, one shadow of doubt. Her breath caught when she found only determination and complete commitment.

And what a heady mixture that was. So heady she nearly climaxed right there and then without so much as a touch.

"So?" he murmured, pressing a searing kiss to the side of her neck. "What do you say, Marie?"

What did she say? All of this was so…new. So unexpected. Never in a million years would she have expected to come home to find Ian sitting waiting for her on her steps. Never would she have thought him capable of laying his emotions bare for her to see and pick over. And never would she have anticipated his proposing to her.

He awkwardly cleared his throat and moved slightly away. Marie wanted to reach out and prevent the move, but she was frozen in place.

"I see," he said quietly.

"Ian..."

He shook his head. "No. That's okay. After what I put you through all these many years, I'd have been surprised if you'd said yes so easily." He skimmed his hand down her arms and gently took her keys from her hand. "Maybe it would help if you met this wise man I spoke of."

Marie stayed right where she was, flush up against the door, staring at him as if he were a stranger—a decadently handsome, full-heartedly frustrating stranger who had stolen her heart—as he put her key in the lock.

The door opened.

"Marie, meet the wise man. Frankie...this is the woman I love."

Marie gasped, staring into the faces of every member of her family. Her father, her mother, her brothers and their wives, and even her grandmother stood in her living room beaming at her like a bunch of coconspirators caught with their hands in the cookie jar.

"A big wedding," her mother said, coming to hug her. "I've been planning it since the day you were born."

Marie stared at Ian's grinning face over the shoulders of her family members as they hugged her. Ian shrugged then crossed his arms as he leaned against the closed door and watched her.

She didn't understand. What was her family doing in her apartment? And what was this wise man thing? And how come none of her brothers were hovering over Ian right now, threatening to pummel him for having sullied their baby sister's reputation?

Finally Marie found herself being pulled into her father's warm, comforting embrace. She stiffened at first, trying to make sense out of the entire scene. Then she melted into the arms of the man who had first held her, and still held her unlike any other man in her life.

Her father leaned back and grinned down at her. "Congratulations, baby."

She slightly shook her head. "But Ian's not Italian...."

He chuckled softly. "No, he's not. He's better. He's the man you love, and the man who loves you."

Her mama put her hands on Marie's shoulders from behind and leaned forward so her cheek rested against her daughter's. "Don't be too upset that we interfered, little one. We just wanted to see you happy."

Frankie Jr. chuckled behind their father. "And happy to the Bertellis means married with lots of kids."

Marie had reached her saturation point about five minutes ago. She looked into all of their faces. "I don't understand."

Her gaze sought and found Ian where he still leaned against the door. "Seems we're the victims of matchmakers."

The laugh that bubbled up from Marie's chest stopped whatever words she might have said as she mentally walked through all the steps leading to this point. Her father's problems. His contacting Ian instead of her. Her cocounseling with Ian. Her brother Frankie Jr. moving in with her.

Okay, maybe that hadn't been orchestrated, but knowing her family and how far they were known to go to get what they wanted, she wouldn't have been the least bit surprised if Frankie and Toni's separation had been a hoax designed to chase her into Ian's arms.

"A May wedding," her grandmother said in her thickly accented voice. "That will give us enough time to put everything in motion."

Ian cleared his throat. "She hasn't said yes yet."

Every eye in the room turned to stare at her in shock, making her want to dive for the nearest door. Unfortunately, Ian happened to be blocking it.

She stuck out her chin. "A girl is entitled to take her time in matters of this nature," she said. "In fact, I don't think I'll have an answer for at least…well, two seconds." She grinned at Ian, blinking twice, then said, "Yes. Yes, Ian Kilborn, I'll marry you."

Epilogue

IF ONLY MARIE HAD KNOWN right away that her grand-mother had meant May as in three months away, not May as in the following year, she might have been able to put a stop to it. But by the time she'd caught on, the invitations to Italian relatives had been mailed and the church reserved and her family had hijacked her life yet again, filling her time off with detail after detail of her wedding planning and the search for the house she and Ian planned to live in after they were married, so that she and Ian had very little time alone.

Of course, it didn't help that she had landed a very important case last month, and Ian had just been pro-moted to full partner at his law firm, either.

Even today, a Sunday morning when she should be lolling about in bed with Ian recovering from a fantas-tic night of sex, her mother had invited them and Dulcy and Jena and their husbands to lunch to discuss the wedding.

All things considered, Marie would much rather be in bed with her fiancé.

Her fiancé...

She shivered all over, feeling sexy and needy and yet complete.

Unfortunately, Ian's being her fiancé meant she saw even less of him now than before, and it was frustrating as hell.

She made a sharp sound of frustration as she put the pitcher of lemonade down on the table of her parents' back balcony, then smiled at Dulcy and Jena who were watching their men, Quinn and Tommy, try to help Ian put together a wooden gym set in the backyard some thirty feet away.

Jena sighed and put her feet up on the chair Tommy had vacated a half hour ago. "It all looks so…domestic, doesn't it?"

"Wonderfully so." Dulcy laughed as she caressed her growing belly. At eight months, she was bigger than Marie had ever thought possible and looked about ready to pop at any moment. Not that you could tell by looking at her. She looked happy and, as impossible as it seemed, sexy as hell.

She heard a shout and looked to find Ian shaking his hand where he must have hit it with a hammer. Frustration, it seemed, was eating away at him, as well.

"You know you two could always elope," Jena suggested.

Marie stared at her. "You're joking, right? My family would hang us both from that tree over there."

"So don't tell them."

She looked at Dulcy, surprised the words had come from her traditional mouth. Then again, how traditional was she when she'd ended up marrying her ex-groom's best man?

Jena sighed again. "Oh, yes. I definitely should have paid more attention while we were all growing up."

Marie followed her friend's gaze back to Ian then gaped at her friend in disbelief.

"What?" Jena said, all innocent. "Had I known the guy would have grown up to be so utterly edible I would have been a little nicer to him, that's all."

"You have your own man," Marie said.

The words played out through her mind again. It seemed all three of them now had their own men. In Dulcy's case, she'd ended up with a different man than with what she started. In Jena's, she'd been outwitted by a man who had found out where she lived. And she...

Marie caught herself smiling.

Well, she had finally caught the man it seemed she'd been chasing after all her life. While their courtship had taken a circuitous route, it had ended up back where it had all began, making her the happiest—if the most frustrated—woman on Earth.

Well, okay. Maybe one of three of the happiest women on Earth.

Ian caught her gaze, the provocative suggestion his eyes making her feel warmer than the spring sunshine.

And until they got married, there was always the pantry...

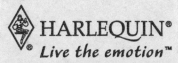

THE BAD GIRLS Club

They're strong, they're sexy, they're not afraid to use the assets Mother Nature gave them....

Venus Messina is...

#916 WICKED & WILLING
by Leslie Kelly
February 2003

Sydney Colburn is...

#920 BRAZEN & BURNING
by Julie Elizabeth Leto
March 2003

Nicole Bennett is...

#924 RED-HOT & RECKLESS
by Tori Carrington
April 2003

The Bad Girls Club...where membership has its privileges!

Available wherever

HARLEQUIN®

Temptation.

is sold....

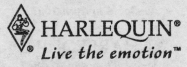

HARLEQUIN®

Live the emotion™

Visit us at www.eHarlequin.com

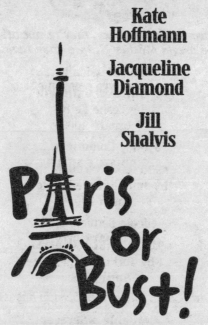

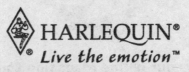